LETTERS
FROM SARAH

What Reviewers Say About
Joy Argento's Work

Exes and O's

"I really appreciated the new take on a burned lover in Ali. Instead of pushing love away forever, she decides to actively seek out what has gone wrong in order to do better in her future. I also enjoyed how the story focuses on what a healthy relationship should be and how to get to that. It was refreshing. ...If you're in the mood for a gentle second-chance romance that has just enough angst, great character development, and will have you dying for a donut, run for this book!"—*Lesbian Review*

Before Now

"*Before Now* by Joy Argento is a mixture of modern day romance and historical fiction. ...There was some welcome humour and a bit of angst. An interesting story well told."—*Kitty Kat's Book Review Blog*

Emily's Art and Soul

"...the leads are well rounded and credible. As a 'friends to lovers' romance the author skillfully transforms their budding friendship to an increasing intimacy. Mindy, Emily's Down syndrome sister, is a great secondary character, very realistic in her traits and interactions with other people. Her fresh outlook on life and her 'best friend' declarations help to keep the upbeat tone."—*LezReviewBooks*

"This was such a sweet book. Great story that would be perfect as a holiday read. The plot was fun and the pace really good. The protagonists were enjoyable and Emily's character was well fleshed out. …This is the first book I've read by Joy Argento and it won't be the last. I'm looking forward to what comes next."
—*Rainbow Literary Society*

Taking the Plunge by Amanda Radley. When Regina Avery meets model Grace Holland—the most beautiful woman she's ever seen—she doesn't have a clue how to flirt, date, or hold on to a relationship. But Regina must take the plunge with Grace and hope she manages to swim. (978-1-63679-400-6)

We Met in a Bar by Claire Forsythe. Wealthy nightclub owner Erica turns undercover bartender on a mission to catch a thief where she meets no-strings, no-commitments Charlie, who couldn't be further from Erica's type. Right? (978-1-63679-521-8)

Western Blue by Suzie Clarke. Step back in time to this historic western filled with heroism, loyalty, friendship, and love. The odds are against this unlikely group—but never underestimate women who have nothing to lose. (978-1-63679-095-4)

Windswept by Patricia Evans. The windswept shores of the Scottish Highlands weave magic for two people convinced they'd never fall in love again. (978-1-63679-382-5)

Visit us at www.boldstrokesbooks.com

By the Author

Emily's Art and Soul

Before Now

Carrie and Hope

No Regrets

Exes and O's

Missed Conception

Gin and Bear It

I Do, I Don't

Letters from Sarah

LETTERS FROM SARAH

by

Joy Argento

2024

LETTERS FROM SARAH
© 2024 By Joy Argento. All Rights Reserved.

ISBN 13: 978-1-63679-509-6

This Trade Paperback Original Is Published By
Bold Strokes Books, Inc.
P.O. Box 249
Valley Falls, NY 12185

First Edition: January 2024

Credits
Editor: Cindy Cresap
Production Design: Susan Ramundo
Cover Design By Tammy Seidick and Joy Argento

Acknowledgments

I would like to thank the readers who have taken the time to read my books and leave reviews. Your support has kept my fingers moving across the keyboard spitting out stories that would have made my brain explode if they didn't come out. Thanks for keeping my head intact.

Thank you to my editor, Cindy Cresap. Your words of encouragement mean the world to me.

Special thanks to Olessia Butenko, Julie Spelman, and Tobie Hewitt for finding all the mistakes that I miss. I am so grateful for you.

Thank you to my support system. You keep me going.
Susan Carmen-Duffy
Karin Cole
Barbara DiFiore
And my kids, Jamie, Jess, and Tony

CHAPTER ONE

Sarah Osborn hit send on her laptop and watched the email disappear from the screen as it traveled through cyberspace to no one. The tears that cascaded down her cheeks dripped onto the keyboard, and she swiped at them with a tissue before wiping her eyes.

She'd done it. It was harder than she thought, but she'd survived so much heartache over the last two years, and she would survive this too. This was a step forward. A step she needed to take in order to get on with her life. A life that she hadn't been living. Not really. Yes, she went to work Monday through Friday. But weekends and evenings had mostly been spent alone on the couch bingeing mindless TV shows.

She got the occasional call from a family member or friend, checking up on her and inviting her to dinner or some random party. The more she said no, the more the invitations dried up, until they all but disappeared. It was pretty much just her immediate family that extended invitations these days. That was on her and she was determined to change it. She'd taken the first step by sending the email. The next step was rediscovering a social life. Easier said than done.

She closed the laptop, set it on the coffee table, and headed up the stairs. She opened the door to her art studio, a revamped bedroom in her two-story house—a house that seemed much too big to her now. "What a mess," she said out loud. The room had become a dump all for everything and anything she didn't want to look at or think about. And there had been a lot of it. She opened one of the three large plastic bins she'd purchased from Walmart and tossed the cover aside. It didn't take long for the bin to be filled, mostly with clothes. She took a shirt back out of the bin, brought it up to her face and breathed in. She wasn't sure if she was disappointed or relieved that it no longer smelled like Julie. Probably a little of both.

She lugged the bin down the stairs and loaded it into the back of her car to drop off at the thrift store after work. She filled the other two bins and left them by the top of the stairs. She would take care of them later. There was still a lot of stuff she needed to go through, and she briefly considered packing it in garbage bags to throw out. No. It was hard enough donating it. Throwing it out would break her heart.

She moved it all to one corner and threw a blanket that she retrieved from her bedroom closet over the pile. Out of sight, out of mind. Well, that was the theory anyway. She could pick up more bins on the weekend to finish the job.

With that out of the way, she turned to the real task at hand. A quick inventory of her art supplies told her she had almost everything she needed. A few new paintbrushes and some more canvases would be easy enough to get at the local art store.

She wiped the dust off her desktop computer and fired it up. It took longer to turn on than she remembered. Two clicks later, the folder of reference pictures opened. Scrolling through them brought a flood of emotions. There were plenty of still life arrangements, vases of flowers, apples and pears, teacups, and such. Julie had helped with most of the arrangements.

She shed less tears than she expected and roughly wiped away any that escaped her eyes. After going through most of the photos, she moved ten of them to a new folder that she named *Next*.

With a clean canvas on her easel, she turned off the light and shut the door. She had ten paintings to produce in the next three months. Cleaning the room was a good start. She hoped that the muse would accompany her on this journey. She'd pushed her away for two years. Sarah couldn't blame her if she never returned.

❖

"Whatcha doing?"

Lindsey Cooper looked up from her lunch at Cricket who could only be seen from the nose up as she looked over the side of Lindsey's cubicle. Lindsey wondered how she could even see over the top of it. It had to be a good two inches above her head.

"Are you standing on a step stool?" Lindsey asked.

"It is a step stool. I never knew my real stool. This one adopted me when I was a baby."

"You're a nut." Lindsey laughed. "You know that?"

"I don't know who my real parents are. But that's okay. My step stool treated me like her own."

Cricket disappeared and reappeared with her feet on the ground coming around the side of the cubicle wall. She pointed at Lindsey's lunch. "How can you eat just salad? I'd be starving all day."

"I happen to like salad."

Cricket perched a hip on Lindsey's desk. They'd been friends since middle school when Lindsey threatened to beat up a bully who was teasing Cricket. She was so relieved when the bully, Janet Jacobson, backed down. Lindsey's threat was empty and if faced with fighting or fleeing she would have hightailed it out of there like she was on fire. She heard that Janet had become a nun after high school. Who would have thunk it? To this day, Lindsey was grateful to Janet for bringing her and Cricket together. Cricket had been her rock through all the ups and downs in life. Especially when Lindsey's girlfriend broke up with her nine months ago, with no warning.

"Liar. No one likes salad. They like the dressing. The ooey gooey dressing."

"True. But we can't all have a killer figure like you without watching what we eat."

"There is nothing wrong with your figure, lady. A little ice cream now and then wouldn't hurt you."

Lindsey didn't bother telling her she'd had a bowl of rocky road the night before. That was why she was eating a salad for lunch. Not that it would have mattered. She told Cricket just about everything.

"How come you're not eating?" Lindsey asked.

"I'm leaving early today." She tossed her long dark hair over her shoulder. "I have to get ready for my date tonight."

"Oh yeah. The famous Dr. Manly."

Cricket laughed. "Dr. Manning. You know how long I've had a crush on him."

Lindsey tapped her chin. "Yes. Since nineteen thirty-two, I believe."

"At least." Cricket grabbed a cherry tomato from Lindsey's salad and popped it into her mouth.

"What are you going to wear?"

"Is showing up naked too obvious?"

"I do believe it is."

They spent the next ten minutes discussing the pros and cons of a dress versus slacks and pumps versus flats. They had reached no definite conclusions by the time Cricket left. She promised to send Lindsey a selfie showing what she decided on and a full report the next day.

Lindsey was happy but a little envious that Cricket was going on a date with someone she'd been interested in for a long time. There hadn't been anyone who sparked Lindsey's interest like that since her relationship ended. She was open to the idea—maybe more than open—to another relationship. She missed being in love and having a person that was just hers. Sure, she did stuff with Cricket, but it wasn't the same.

She finished her lunch, put the container back into her backpack, and turned her attention to her computer. She still had five minutes left on her lunch break so she checked her personal email—something she would never do on company time.

The amount of spam always surprised and infuriated her. It didn't seem to matter how much she adjusted her settings, tons of it made it into her main account instead of her spam folder. She deleted ten emails and was about to delete the next one when she stopped. It wasn't for some pill to give her a bigger penis—something she obviously didn't need, or some offer for a new credit card. She didn't recognize the sender. The subject line read *My Love*. That certainly piqued her interest. She opened the email and was surprised to see it was addressed to someone named Julie.

My dear Julie,

I hope this email finds you at peace and surrounded by love. I miss you more every day, and the pain of losing you is still so raw. I want to let you know that I've been doing a lot of thinking and soul-searching lately. I know you would want me to be happy and to live my life to the fullest. And, although it feels like a betrayal to even consider moving on, I know I need to.

I'm still figuring out what this means for me and what the future holds. But I want to thank you for being the love of my life and for all the memories we shared together. You have left an indelible mark on my heart, and I will carry you with me always. I hope you can forgive me for taking this step forward and that you understand that this is not good-bye, but rather a new chapter in my life. I will love you forever.

Love always,
Sarah

Lindsey felt like she'd invaded someone's privacy and deepest thoughts by reading the email intended for someone else. She also felt her heart ping for the author of those thoughts. Whoever this Julie was, she was obviously loved deeply by Sarah. She also didn't appear to be in Sarah's life anymore. Lindsey could feel Sarah's pain in those words.

Lindsey knew all too well what it was like to have someone she loved leave her. Sarah loved Julie enough to let her go and wish her well. Lindsey hadn't been able to do that when her girlfriend, Tina, left her. She apparently wasn't as big a person as Sarah was. Lindsey had wanted to do nothing more than track Tina down and punch her in the face. Yes, she still loved Tina when they broke up—loved her for months afterward—but she hated her too. Hated how much she hurt her. Hated how she'd left Lindsey when things seemed so good between them. Hated how Tina had found someone else so soon after they broke up. Hated how much she missed her.

She wondered how Sarah could be so kind and forgiving. It was something worth thinking about. Did she still hold resentment toward Tina? Had she forgiven her? She wasn't sure. She didn't think about her often, but when she did it no longer caused a surge of acid in her stomach. It didn't bring up any emotion at all. Yes, she was pretty sure she had forgiven her. Obviously, the relationship hadn't been as good for Tina as it had been for Lindsey. So, could she really blame her for leaving? She was still pondering the question when she realized her lunch break was over.

She clicked on *Save email as new* and closed her personal account. She would respond to Sarah's email at home and explain how it ended up in her inbox by mistake. That way at least Sarah could make sure it was resent to the right person.

She opened the spreadsheet on her computer and went over the information she'd input before her lunch break. As much as she tried to concentrate on her work, her mind returned again and again to Sarah's email. She felt for her, her pain, her loss, her kindness. She concluded that Sarah must be an exceptional person to send such an email. She vowed to be more like that.

Not that she didn't consider herself kind. She did. Her friends told her as much. But extending that kindness, even if it was only in her thoughts, to Tina as Sarah did with Julie wouldn't be a bad thing.

The rest of the workday seemed to drag on forever. At two minutes after five, she turned her computer off, grabbed her backpack and her jacket, and headed out the door. Most days she hung around after work and chatted with Cricket before heading out. She was grateful that Cricket had left early. She wasn't in much of a chatting mood for some reason.

It was much warmer out than when she'd walked to work that morning. She flung the jacket over her shoulder, raised her chin, eyes closed, for a moment and let the sun warm her face. The early spring weather was perfect. She often walked the half-mile to work when the weather permitted. She'd attempted it a few times in the winter, but the cold chilled her to the bone, as Western New York weather was known to do.

Her phone pinged with a text as she unlocked her door. She put a fresh bowl of water down for her cat, Maximus, ignoring her phone in the moment. He rubbed up against her legs as way of greeting. She'd learned to wait until he was done before moving. He tended to weave in and around her legs a few times and she didn't want to risk tripping, or worse, stepping on him. He sauntered off, most likely to lie in the living room in the pool of sunshine pouring in through the bay window. That window was one of the first things that attracted Lindsey to the house when she decided to move out of the apartment she shared with Tina, two months after Tina left. Life as a homeowner was a little more challenging than she expected—the lawn needed to be mowed often, and something was always in need of repair. But she loved her home—her own little piece of paradise—with its long driveway, built in bookcases, and a front porch the entire length of the house. The master bedroom wasn't much bigger than the two guest rooms. One was set up for Cricket when she slept over and the other was for her plants. Currently she had five fig cuttings that she was trying to root. She was hoping to get at least one to grow big enough so she could plant it in the yard.

She checked on the plants, sticking her finger into the dirt in each pot to see if any needed water. None did. She resisted the temptation to check the clear plastic cups with the fig cuttings. She'd only started them the week before and they probably wouldn't show any signs of roots for at least a month.

After settling down on the couch, she pulled her phone from her back pocket and opened her text messages. There were several pictures of Cricket wearing different outfits.

Which one did you pick? Lindsey texted.

It took a few minutes for Cricket's reply to come through. *Guess.*

Lindsey scrolled back through the pictures. *The blue blouse with the gray slacks?*

You are sooooo good! Cricket responded.

I got it right?

Hell no. I'm wearing the lavender dress. I meant just in general you're good. And smart. And pretty. And kind. And did I happen to mention good?

I believe you did. I hope you have a wonderful time tonight. You deserve it!

Cricket sent a smiley face, a heart, a glass of wine, and an eggplant emoji back.

Lindsey laughed and tossed her phone next to her. She grabbed her laptop from the coffee table in front of her and fired it up. To her surprise there was another email from Sarah addressed to Julie.

Dear Julie,

I bet you didn't expect to hear from me again so soon. Sometimes I feel so lost without you. I have such mixed feelings as I am preparing for my upcoming art show. On one hand, I am happy (as happy as I can be without you) to be showcasing my work and sharing it with the world again. On the other hand, I cannot help but feel a deep sadness knowing that you will not be there to share in this experience with me like you always did in the past. I'll miss not having you there to hold my hand and calm my nerves. You were always so much better at talking to people than I was. I'm not sure how to do this without you reassuring me that I can.

I think of you often, and the memories we shared together still bring a smile to my face. You were always so supportive of my passion for art, and I can only imagine how proud you would be of me right now. Your absence is felt every day, but especially so on special occasions like this.

Please know that you are always in my thoughts and that I am so sorry that you cannot be here to see my work on display. I wish more than anything that you could be, not only at my art opening but in my life again. In my (our) home. In my bed. I think that is when I miss you most. I turn over and you're not there.

I said that I'm ready to move on and I mean it. I won't keep emailing you, but I don't think I'll ever stop talking to you in my heart. That is where you still reside and always will. I am filled with a sense of gratitude and appreciation for all the support and love you gave me during our time together. Your encouragement and belief in me gave me the strength to pursue my dreams, and I will always be grateful for that.

I am sending you love and light, and I hope that you can feel my thoughts and words are with you always.

With love and sadness,
Sarah

"Wow," Lindsey said out loud. Maximus jumped up on the couch next to her. She turned her attention to the cat. "Is it stupid that I think this woman is wonderful?"

Maximus blinked at her.

"I mean the only thing I know is that she's some sort of an artist and that this Julie character left her. I'm assuming that means she's a lesbian."

Maximus yawned, turned in a circle, and settled himself down resting his back against her.

"Yep. You're right. It is stupid. Okay. Let me just send her a quick note to let her know her emails aren't getting to Julie." She hit the reply button and began to type.

CHAPTER TWO

Sarah put her paintbrush down and took several steps back. This was the third day she'd worked on the painting, and she wasn't sure if she liked it or not. It had been so long since she'd painted that she felt like she might have forgotten how. It wasn't like riding a bike where muscle memory took over. This was more than that. This was calling on her creativity, her brain, her eyes, her hand, her heart. That was what was missing. Her heart.

Four hours of painting had made her back sore. She put her hands on her hips and stretched from side to side to try to loosen it up. It might be better to work sitting down, she decided. But enough for now, she cleaned her brushes, covered her palette, and washed her hands.

Down in the kitchen, she peered into the refrigerator. Nothing looked appealing, but the growl from her stomach told her that skipping dinner wasn't an option. She found a box of corn flakes in the pantry. She wasn't sure how long ago she bought it, but it hadn't been opened so it was probably fine. The milk was fresh from her grocery shopping the day before. Two spoonfuls of sugar sprinkled on top and her dinner was ready. Julie wouldn't approve. But then again Julie would have been the one cooking dinner.

After her filling but unsatisfying dinner, Sarah retrieved her laptop and headed up the stairs. She changed for bed and brushed her teeth. She piled up the pillows, pulled back the covers, and climbed in, sitting up with her laptop perched on her legs. She watched a couple of YouTube videos on oil painting trying to refresh her memory and find inspiration.

She turned on the TV and opened her email, which she'd neglected for the last few days. If her heart could have stopped it would have. There was an email from Julie. How was that possible? She stared at the subject line *Re: My Love*. Her fingers trembled as she clicked on it.

Hi Sarah,

You don't know me, but I received a couple of emails from you that were meant for someone else, and I wanted to reach out to let you know. I understand how easily mistakes like this can happen, and I want to apologize if this has caused any discomfort or inconvenience for you. I know this was meant to be a private message to Julie.

I have to say your emails touched my heart. I too was left by someone I loved. I know this is strange, but if you ever need anyone to talk to who has been there, let me know.

If there's anything else I can do for you, please don't hesitate to reach out.

Best regards,
Lindsey

It wasn't from Julie. Of course, it wasn't. How could it be? Julie was gone. Either she had messed up or someone else had Julie's old email address. Either way, this Lindsey person had read the email she sent to her wife—her wife who had lost her life two years ago when a tractor trailer lost control on a hill and slammed into Julie's car, sending Julie into eternity.

Lindsey had gotten the email intended for Julie's soul. Not that Sarah had actually expected Julie to get it. It wasn't that she didn't believe in an afterlife. She did. It was that she found it cathartic to put down in words her message to Julie, which, in a way, was also a message to herself. She wasn't sure how she felt about someone else—Lindsey—reading it.

She read the email again. Lindsey seemed kind, not intrusive like Sarah first thought. She offered an ear if Sarah needed to talk. Apparently, Lindsey had also lost someone. Her family had suggested several times that Sarah join a grief support group. They thought it might be a way for Sarah to get her life back on track. But the thought of sitting in a group of people that oozed sadness—like she suspected she did—wasn't something she was willing to do. But emailing another woman who knew the heartbreak of loss might not be a bad idea.

The fact that she was entertaining the idea of corresponding with this woman surprised her. What could it hurt? If it didn't feel right, she could always stop. She would have to think about this.

How had the email ended up in Lindsey's inbox? She was pretty sure the email address would have had to have been closed in order for someone else to use it. It looked right to her, not that she had emailed Julie often—mostly just forwarding an interesting article or some idea she thought Julie would be interested in. She wondered if Julie's parents had somehow managed to close it. She hadn't talked to them since the funeral. It was too painful.

She made her way to her art room and opened the desk drawer. She found the pad of paper with her random notes. On the third page, in Julie's handwriting, was her email address. There was the answer. Sarah had forgotten that it ended in nineteen-eighty, the year Julie was born. *Well, that was stupid of me.* But if Lindsey turned out to be someone she could correspond with—someone who understood the loss Sarah felt—it might have been a mistake that was meant to be. Sarah used to believe such things—that there were no coincidences. But somewhere along the line she'd forgotten that. She'd forgotten much of her spiritual beliefs since Julie left her life. It might be time for a refresher. She not only needed to get back to her beliefs but also to herself. She had somehow managed to lose herself when she lost Julie. It was as if Julie had taken huge chunks of Sarah when she left this earth.

She knew she needed to find those parts of herself and get them back. It was time. She went back to her bed and opened her laptop. This time she typed in the correct email address and started another email to Julie.

My love,

My last two emails to you went to someone else. Not that I expected them to reach you in the heavens and beyond. If you were here right now, I know you would shake your head and laugh. You loved it when I screwed up, saying I appeared to be human like the rest of the world. For some strange reason, you seemed to have put me on a pedestal. Your leaving me knocked me to the ground. But enough of that. I am picking myself up and dusting myself off—and I seem to be very dusty. I won't reiterate what I said in my other two misdirected emails. Someone named Lindsey got them and she offered to chat with me. She said she lost someone too, so she probably understands. I think you would want this for me. So tomorrow morning I'll answer her email—you know me, I need time to figure out what to say. Wish me luck.

All my heart,
Sarah

Sarah closed her laptop and scrolled through the channels on the TV, looking for something mindless to watch. It had become a habit. A way to escape the pain. But tonight, for some reason—maybe that reason was Lindsey—she didn't feel pain. She felt hope. She turned the TV off and went back into her art room.

She lowered the painting on her easel, sat in her office chair, and pulled it up to her artwork. She studied her reference picture for a few minutes, compared it to her painting, and decided what to do next. It was close to midnight by the time she cleaned her brushes and went back to bed. She was grateful and a little surprised the muse had shown up and guided her and was pleased with what she had accomplished. The painting was definitely taking shape.

She thought about Lindsey's email and offer to chat as she lay in bed. Possible responses ran through her like a movie script, and she was unable to settle on one. Whatever she decided on, she was looking forward to Lindsey's response. Which was just plain strange and a little disconcerting. It had been so long since she'd looked forward to anything.

❖

Cricket popped into Lindsey's cubicle. "Have you heard back from the mysterious Sarah?"

Lindsey had told her how she'd gotten the emails by mistake and how she felt for the woman and the pain she was obviously going through, and how she offered to help if Sarah wanted it. She left out the fact that she really wanted Sarah to take her up on the offer and the opportunity to get to know her. That sounded a little creepy even in her own mind. "I have not. No big deal." Was she trying to convince Cricket or herself? Probably both. She swung her backpack over her shoulder, grabbed her jacket from the back of her chair, and headed outside, followed by Cricket.

Rain pelted her face as she stepped out the door. Damn. She hadn't bothered checking the weather report before walking to work that morning, so, of course, she didn't have an umbrella.

"Want a ride home?" Cricket asked, as if reading her mind.

"That would be great."

Cricket turned around. "Hop on. We'll piggyback it."

Lindsey laughed. "I was hoping we could use your car. It might save you from going to the chiropractor."

"Good thinking. I knew I kept you around for a reason."

"I thought it was my magnetic personality and unbelievable charm."

"Well, there is that." Crickey pressed the button on her key fob as they approached her car and unlocked the doors.

A small trickle of water ran through Lindsey's hair and down her forehead. She wiped it away before sliding onto the leather seat. They were in Lindsey's driveway in a matter of minutes. "Want to come in? I have a bottle of wine with your name on it."

"Ah yes. Cricket wine. My favorite. But I'm going to pass."

"Another date with the fab doctor? What is this, like three nights in a row?"

"It is. I'm starting to think he likes me. And who knows, I may get lucky tonight."

"He would be the lucky one." Lindsey reached across the seat and gave Cricket a squeeze. "Thanks for the ride. I hope your date goes great." She smiled and added. "Don't do anything I wouldn't do."

"Hell no, I'm not listening to that advice. You wouldn't sleep with a man, so no." She wagged her finger. "I'm gonna do exactly what you wouldn't do."

Lindsey laughed. "I love you. Do everything I wouldn't do." She opened the car door and sprinted to her house as the rain picked up. She was greeted at the door by Maximus—greeted so intensely that she almost tripped over him. Maximus let out a loud meow of protest as if she was the one who had been in the wrong.

"Excuse me," Lindsey said, feigning indignity. "You were in my way. Not the other way around." She scooped him up in her arms, but he wiggled free. "One minute you love me, the next, not so much. Typical."

She ordered her dinner from Grubhub—Chinese—from her favorite place—and turned the TV on while she waited. She avoided checking her email. The hundred or so times she'd checked it in the past few days proved fruitless. She was pretty sure at this point that Sarah—kind of weird to refer to her as if she were a friend—wasn't ever going to answer her. She wasn't sure she would either given the same situation. There were so many scammers out there that you didn't know who to believe anymore.

Her food came in record time, and she tipped the driver an extra five dollars. She ate at the small kitchen table she'd inherited from her grandmother and added a glass of chardonnay. She promised herself when she got her first apartment after college that she wouldn't sit in front of the television to eat her meals. She was able to keep that promise—mostly. It had been harder to do since Tina up and left. She'd allowed herself several weeks to indulge in the sin of living room eating along with plenty of self-pity and of course hate. The kind of hate reserved only for someone you loved.

But that was in the past. It took months, but she was back to her old routine and the hate had subsided to indifference. Any love that lingered was only for a few select memories. She wasn't quite ready for full on dating yet but had allowed herself a few random nights with strangers. It was more satisfying than what she could accomplish on her own but just barely. She was the type that wanted—no—needed a connection with someone for the sex to be fulfilling.

A load of laundry, two chapters in a romance novel—why did she love that stuff, it never happened that way in real life— and fresh food for Maximus later, she headed to bed. One last look at her email on her phone and... Wait. There it was. An email from Sarah. Was it possible that her heart actually skipped a beat? Another thing that only happened in books.

She sat up in bed and took a breath. What the hell? Sarah was a stranger who seemed to have compassion for her ex. She wasn't royalty or a celebrity. Why was Lindsey so drawn in by her? It didn't make sense. She braced herself for a simple *thanks for your email, have a nice life* response.

She was surprised by the length of it at first glance. It was obviously more than a *kiss-off* letter. She threw the phone on the bed next to her and retrieved her laptop from the living room, bringing it back to bed with her.

She rearranged her pillows so she could sit up, leaned against them, and opened the email.

Dear Lindsey,

I hope this letter finds you well. It meant so much to me that you took the time to let me know my email landed in your inbox by mistake. Not everyone would have done that. I also wanted to take a moment to express my gratitude for your offer to help me deal with the grief of losing my wife. Losing someone, as you know, is never easy. Your kind words and willingness to listen have touched my heart. Grief is a journey that never seems to end, although there are times when the pain seems to wane only to come back full force and knock the wind out of me. Julie and I were together for fifteen years, married for ten. She died a little over two years ago. It was sudden and left a hole that has—had— taken over my life. Other than work—I'm an executive at Petty Finance—I pretty much shut down. As you undoubtedly gleaned from my emails, I'm stepping back into life. It's time.

I have a friend who owns an art gallery and had offered me my own show in a few months. Of course, it's like the millionth time she offered, but up until now I've turned her down.

I oil paint and hadn't done it since losing Julie. I am proud to say I've picked my brushes back up and gotten myself back to work. My first painting in a long time is almost done. Only nine more to go.

Please tell me more about you and the person you lost. Death is such a permanent thing. I would like to offer you the same thing you were kind enough to offer me, an ear to listen, even if it's only through email, although I'm not opposed to talking on the phone at some point if you're interested.

I know all this seems strange. At least it does to me. You get an email from a stranger and offer a hand. Said stranger responds with a hand of her own. Who knows, maybe we can be friends. I seemed to have misplaced most of mine when my grief got in the way.

Once again, thank you from the bottom of my heart for your
kindness and generosity. I look forward to hearing back from you.

With warm regards,
Sarah

"Holy crap," Lindsey said. "It wasn't a breakup. Sarah's
wife died. And she thinks my person died too." How was Sarah
going to feel when she learned that Lindsey's grief came from
Tina leaving her? Her pain paled in comparison to Sarah's. She
wasn't sure how to respond to the email.

If she told her that she didn't have someone close to her die,
at least not in the way Sarah had, would Sarah still be interested
in talking? Losing her grandmother wasn't the same. And Tina
walking out on her certainly wasn't either.

"Well, I guess that's that," she said. She was sure Sarah wasn't
going to want to bother with her when she found out that all was not
equal. She closed the lid on her laptop and laid it next to her. She'd
answer the email in the next day or two. She briefly considered
dancing around the fact that Tina left and didn't die but decided
against it. That wouldn't be fair to anyone, especially Sarah. The
last thing she wanted was to cause Sarah any more pain.

"Why didn't you answer her?" Cricket asked Lindsey the
next day.

"I don't know. I guess I feel *less than*."

"What does that mean?" Cricket leaned her hip against
Lindsey's desk.

"Her wife died. Tina left me. It's not the same. I'm not
sure I have anything to offer her. I thought we had something in
common."

"Pain is pain, Lindsey. You seemed intrigued by this woman.
You should answer her email and see what she says. Worst that
can happen is she doesn't want to continue talking. But who
knows, you just might make a friend." Cricket helped herself to
a potato chip from Lindsey's lunch and popped it in her mouth.

"I guess you're right."

"Oh my God. Don't you know by now that I'm always right?"

Lindsey shook her head. "I just forget sometimes. On a different note, how did your date go last night? Was the good doctor—well—good?"

Cricket laughed. "Good kisser. Beyond that I don't know. Seems he is quite the gentleman. We talked about it and decided to wait a bit. Get to know each other. It was quite a change from the guys I've dated lately who only want one thing."

"Are you okay with that? I mean I know you wanted to take it to the next level."

"The disappointment was replaced by…" Cricket seemed to think about it for several long moments. "I don't know. Replaced by respect. It only makes me want him more." She placed her hand over Lindsey's. "I really want this one to work."

Lindsey felt the sincerity in her words. "I want that for you, too."

Cricket glanced at Lindsey's computer screen. "You have fifteen minutes left on your lunch break. Write that email. Let me know how it goes." She slipped quietly out of Lindsey's cubicle.

Lindsey finished her sandwich, turned her attention to her computer, and started typing.

CHAPTER THREE

"Well, shit," Sarah said as she read Lindsey's email. "Guess we don't have as much in common as I thought." She continued reading. "I know our pain isn't the same. I assumed it was. I'm sorry about that. I would love to continue communicating if you're interested. I'm a great listener."

There was something about Lindsey that was captivating even if she hadn't gone through the same kind of grief as Sarah. What was the harm in making a new friend? A friend that Sarah knew very little about other than she was obviously gay, and her girlfriend broke her heart leaving it in pieces. Lindsey seemed to have been able to put most of those pieces back together. In her email she'd also mentioned that she was a market researcher, not that Sarah knew what that meant, and that she would love to see pictures of Sarah's art show when it was set up.

Sarah sent an email back.

Dear Lindsey,

Thanks for your email and your honesty. I do have to admit that like you, I assumed we'd both had the same kind of loss. And even though Tina left you and didn't die, I could still sense your pain through your words. I feel like we have a lot in common. It's clear to me that we've both experienced significant grief and loss in our lives, and I think that gives us a unique perspective on the world.

I've been thinking about ways we could support each other, and I wanted to suggest that we get to know each other better. How would you feel about texting or even a phone call?

In the meantime, I wanted to share a picture of the painting I'm currently working on. It needs at least one more layer, maybe two, but it needs to dry completely in between, and with oil paints that can take some time. I've attached a photo of it to this email.

Anyway, I just wanted to say that I hope we can continue our chats and get to know each other better. I'm looking forward to hearing back from you.

Take care,
Sarah

She added her phone number after her name and pressed send.

She considered going up to her art room to continue working on her painting but opted to let it dry one more day. At least that's what she told herself. The reality was she was tired after her day at work, and creativity wasn't easy to access when she felt like this. She retrieved her phone from the kitchen table and hit her sister Mary's contact number.

"Hey, Sarah," her sister said. "Everything alright?"

"Yes. Why are you starting the conversation that way?"

Her sister paused. "Um…well…I don't remember the last time you called me. I mean, I know we talk, but I'm usually the one that calls you."

Sarah knew she had withdrawn from mostly everyone in the last couple of years but hadn't realized it was so obvious to other people. "Yeah. Sorry about that. I'm trying to step out into the world again. Wondered if maybe you wanted to catch a movie, maybe dinner first."

"You sure you're alright?"

"Stop asking me that. I'm fine."

"Okay. I am just finishing cooking supper. Ralph should be home from work any minute. How would you feel about joining us and then you and I can go out? Did you have any particular movie in mind?"

Sarah thought about it for few long moments. Ralph was a nice guy. Her sister had met her Prince Charming six years ago and seemed very happy with him. Sarah hadn't gotten together with the two of them since Julie died. She'd seen her sister of course, mostly at their mom's house, but hadn't been to Mary's house in quite some time. It occurred to her just how closed off she'd been. It was time that ended. "Sure. If I leave now, I can be there in ten minutes."

"Great! See you then. And, Sarah…" she let the words trail off.

"Yes?"

"It will be really good to see you."

"It will be good to be seen," Sarah answered and then laughed at how stupid her answer must have sounded. "Hanging up now. See you in a few." She grabbed her coat and drove to her sister's before she had a chance to change her mind. It felt strange to stand at Mary's door and ring the bell. She had almost driven past the house. The last time she was here the white house had black trim. It was now cream colored with deep maroon shutters. Sarah liked the change. The narrow flower gardens that lined the sidewalk showed the new life of spring with purple crocuses and the beginning buds of daffodils. Maybe it was a sign. The earth renewed itself every year, it was time she did the same.

"Hey there, stranger." Ralph answered the door and pulled Sarah in for a hug. "I was so happy to hear you were joining us." He stepped back. "Come on in. Mary's in the kitchen." His brown hair was neatly trimmed, as was his beard, and Sarah suspected he'd been to a barber within the last few days. There was just a touch of gray creeping in at the temples. It looked good on him.

Just as Ralph said, Sarah found Mary in the kitchen. She was adding another place setting to the table. "Hi."

Mary turned at the sound of Sarah's voice. "Hi yourself." She crossed the room and gave Sarah a tight squeeze. "I'm glad you're here. Ralph," she said, looking over Sarah's shoulder. "Would you hang Sarah's coat up?"

Sarah slipped out of her jacket and handed it to him. "Thanks." She turned her attention back to Mary. "Anything I can do to help?"

"Nope. Just sit yourself down. Everything is ready. Would you prefer red or white tonight?" Mary had never been a stickler for what kind of wine went with which meal. Sarah appreciated that about her.

"Just water. I haven't had a drink in a long time. I'm afraid it would go right to my head."

"Would that be a bad thing?" Ralph asked as he stepped back into the kitchen.

"It would. I'm trying to get my head right again, and having it float away wouldn't be too good."

"Gotcha. Water it is." He retrieved a glass from the cupboard, filled it with ice and water from the refrigerator door, and set it on the table.

All in all, it turned out to be a nice evening. The dinner was great, as was the movie and the company. It had been far too long since she'd done any real socializing. Neither Mary nor Ralph reprimanded her for staying shut inside herself for so long. She'd had a few friends that had done that, and it left a bad taste in Sarah's mouth. And her heart.

She crawled in bed that night satisfied that she'd taken steps to reestablish her life. She thought briefly about Lindsey before closing her eyes, hoping that she would respond to her email with a phone call or at least a text. She could use a new friend, considering how many she seemed to have lost since Julie died. *Loss* had been her word for the last couple of years. It was time her new word was *gain*. Lindsey seemed, at least from her emails, to be just the right friend to gain. At least Sarah hoped she was.

❖

Lindsey was just about to hang up, sure that the call was going to go Cricket's voice mail, when a breathless Cricket answered.

"Did I catch you at a bad time?" Lindsey asked.

"No. I just left my phone in the kitchen, and I was in the basement doing laundry when I heard it ring. What's up?"

Lindsey hated whenever someone said that to her. Like she needed something to be up for her to call. This time, however, something was up. "I got an email back from Sarah."

"And?"

"And she said she would like to continue talking—"

"That's a good thing, right?" Cricket interrupted her.

"It is, but here's the kicker. She gave me her phone number and it's the same area code as ours. What are the chances? I mean, I figured she was clear across the country or something. I never guessed that she would be so close."

"Wow. That is weird. I think the odds would be one in five hundred. Wait. Be right back." It took several long moments for Cricket to return. "The odds are actually one in three hundred and thirty-five."

"What? How did you come up with that?"

"I googled how many area codes are there in the US of course. But that doesn't account for other countries. I mean we knew she spoke English, but that could have been from any number of other countries. Want me to google how many countries speak English?"

Lindsey shook her head. Sometimes Cricket was off the wall. "No. I don't think we need to know that. You're crazy."

"You've known that for years. I think that's what you love most about me."

"Actually, it is."

"Did you call her yet?"

Lindsey glanced at the clock on her nightstand. "No. I just checked my email a few minutes ago. It's way too late to call now. I think I'm going to start with a text anyway. I'll do it tomorrow." She needed the time to think about what to say anyway. It was one thing to chat with someone that was far away, it was a whole different thing to chat with someone nearby. This made it possible to meet in person. Which, at this point, was something Lindsey hoped might happen.

"Good thinking. Let me know how it goes."

"Absolutely. I'll let you go. I know you want to get back to your laundry. I just wanted to update you."

They said their good-byes. Lindsey plugged her phone in and set it on the nightstand. She thought about all the possible responses to Sarah's email. Suggesting they meet in person so soon probably wasn't a good idea. She didn't want to scare Sarah away. Oh man, she was getting way ahead of herself with this whole thing. Yeah, they'd exchanged a few emails. So why was Sarah so important to her? It didn't make any sense. Was it possible to have such feelings just from someone's emails? From their words? There weren't even *that* many words. It wasn't like they had been emailing each other for years. Hell, it had only been days. Maybe she was just lonely. That would explain a lot. Yeah. That made the most sense. Otherwise, she would have to think she was crazy and crazy wasn't something she wanted to be.

It took her a long time to fall asleep, which was fitful at best. She was sure by the time morning rolled around that she was indeed crazy. It wasn't like her to obsess over anything, let alone a stranger.

She waited until her lunch hour at work to send Sarah a text.

Hi, Sarah. It's Lindsey. Thanks for giving me your phone number. I was surprised to see that we are both in the same area code. I'm in Fairport. I look forward to chatting and getting to know you. You have my number now, so feel free to call or text. I get out of work at 5.

She put her phone on silent and put it in her backpack, so she wasn't tempted to keep checking it. She tried to put it out of her mind. But couldn't. What the hell was wrong with her?

She didn't check her phone until she got home from work and was disappointed to see that Sarah hadn't texted her back. Her phone rang just as she was finishing her supper of tomato soup and a grilled cheese sandwich, a favorite from her childhood. Nothing wrong with comfort food now and then.

It took her a few moments to realize it was Sarah calling. "Stop," she said to her heart that suddenly felt like it was going to burst from her chest and go sprinting down the street. "Hello," she said, into her phone.

"Lindsey?"

"Yes." Way to play it cool.

"Hi. It's Sarah. I hope it's okay that I'm calling."

Lindsey swallowed hard. "Absolutely. I'm so glad you did."

"How are you doing? How was your day?"

At least she didn't say *what's up*. "Fine. Good. Just work and a quick dinner. How are you?"

"Fine as well. I was surprised to find out that we live in the same part of the country. I'm in Webster, so I think we're only about twenty miles apart."

"That's crazy."

"I know. Right?"

There were a few moments of awkward silence. My turn to talk, Lindsey thought. "How are the paintings coming along?" Okay. That was a good question. Lindsey didn't usually have a problem holding an intelligent conversation. Why was she struggling now?

"The first one is almost done. I had a hard time getting it started. I thought it would be like riding a bike, but I guess not." She laughed and Lindsey warmed to the sound of it.

"But you got the hang of it again?"

"I do believe I did. I think it's coming out okay. Would you like to see it?"

"Of course." Was Sarah asking her to come over?

"Hang on. I'll text you a picture. Remember, it isn't finished yet."

Guess it wasn't an invite.

"I sent it. Let me know when you get it."

"Okay." Lindsey heard a ping, indicating a text. She pulled up the picture and was truly impressed. "Wow," she said, even though she didn't have the phone back up to her ear. The painting was of a vase of flowers, sitting next to a window. The natural light poured in and cascaded over the flowers, illuminating them with a soft glow. The glass vase was both transparent and reflective. "Wow," Lindsey repeated, this time into the phone. "That's incredible."

"Thanks. I guess it's okay."

Lindsey was amazed that Sarah didn't seem more pleased with it. "It looks like it's finished to me. What more do you need to do to it?"

Sarah took the time to explain what glazing meant and how the last, thin layer of paint would give the painting more dimension and depth.

"I don't see how it could look better than it already does," Lindsey replied.

"It just gives it that extra umph if you know what I mean. Would you like to come over and see it in person when it's finished?" Sarah couldn't believe she'd just invited Lindsey over. She'd had no intention of doing it when she decided to call her. Lindsey must have thought she was insane inviting a perfect stranger over.

"I would love that."

Maybe Lindsey was as insane as she felt in that moment. Nothing wrong with that. "Great. How about this weekend? It should be done by then."

"That works."

Okay then. Had she really just set up a get-together at her house with this person? Lindsey. Apparently, she had. If nothing else, it would force her to get the painting done. The weekend was only a couple of days away. "How about Sunday?" That would at least give her Saturday to work on it, in case she didn't feel like painting after work.

"Sure," Lindsey said. "Tell me about Julie." Lindsey paused. "I mean if you want to. It seemed obvious from your emails that you loved her very deeply."

It was rare for anyone to ask about Julie. Her friends and even her family avoided the subject as if talking about her would remind Sarah that she was gone. Sarah needed no reminder about that. It was a constant in her life. Julie was gone. That was fact. She appreciated Lindsey asking. "I did—do love her deeply. I'm never sure of the right way to say that."

"I understand. You can still love her even if she's not on this plane anymore."

"Thank you for that. Julie was amazing. So supportive of my art. Very kind but didn't take any shit from anyone." She paused. "Oh sorry. Didn't mean to swear." She tried to watch her language when she was talking to someone new, never knowing how they would react or what they would think of her.

"No problem. I've said that word once or a few hundred times in my life." Lindsey laughed.

"Thanks. Anyway, she was so many contradictory things. I think that's what I loved most about her. She could get down and get dirty and then cleaned up so beautifully."

"She sounds wonderful. I'm sorry I never got to meet her."

That touched Sarah's heart. She spent the next ten minutes talking about Julie, with Lindsey asking questions here and there. It felt good.

They discussed the best time to meet on Sunday and Sarah gave Lindsey the address. They said their good-byes and Sarah hung up. Had that really just happened? She felt a little weird. Not that she expected Lindscy to be anything more than a friend. She wasn't ready for anything more than that. But she hadn't made a new friend in a good many years. And she was looking forward to getting to know this one.

She suddenly felt restless and wasn't sure why. Nothing on the television kept her interest for more than a few minutes as she flipped through the channels. She'd been tired when she got home from work and had planned on going to bed early, but that didn't seem like the best plan anymore. Maybe painting would relax her. It was her own form of meditation. Upstairs in her art room, she studied her work. Yes. One more thin layer would finish it. She gently touched one of the white flower petals to see if it was still wet, knowing that white was one of the slowest drying colors. A bit of paint came off. The rest of the painting seemed dry. She gave it a few moments of thought before deciding not to risk screwing it up by working on it too soon. It surprised her that she was disappointed with this conclusion. She had to force herself to start it and now she was anxious to finish it so she could show it to Lindsey.

CHAPTER FOUR

Lindsey's stomach did a little flip as she rang the doorbell on the two-story colonial house. The trim around the front door was peeling and in need of a new paint job, but the rest of the house looked well cared for.

Shuffling sounds came from inside the house moments before the door was opened. Lindsey had pictured Sarah in her mind from hearing her voice on the phone, but the woman who stood before her was nothing like she'd expected. She appeared to be around the same age as Lindsey, maybe a bit older. Her blond hair was pulled back into a loose ponytail and her bright green eyes were framed by black-rimmed glasses, which Sarah removed from her face and slipped on the top of her head. Pretty, edging toward beautiful was Lindsey's first impression. When a smile spread across Sarah's face, it elevated her looks to full-on gorgeous.

"Lindsey?"

"Hi," Lindsey said. "It's so nice to meet you in person."

Sarah opened her arms for a hug and Lindsey leaned in, happily accepting it. She stood a couple of inches shorter than Lindsey's five foot six.

"Ditto. Come on in."

The house was neat with everything seemingly in its place. The foyer opened to a nice-sized living room with just enough furniture to make it comfortable looking without being overcrowded. The tan couch matched the two chairs and the end tables, oak, Lindsey guessed, matched the coffee table. It was a far cry from Lindsey's mismatched, some new, some thrift store, some hand-me-down furniture.

Sarah gave Lindsey a quick tour of the house before finally landing in the art room. The rest of the house was similar in the style and neatness of the living room.

"Here it is," Sarah said, stepping aside so Lindsey could see the painting, propped up on an easel. It was bigger than Lindsey had imagined but just as beautiful.

"I can't believe you painted this," Lindsey said. She took a couple of steps closer. It was smooth with no discernable brushstrokes. "How do you make it look so real?" She turned toward Sarah and once again took in her features and her smile.

"Patience and very thin layers of paint."

"Are you happy with it?" Lindsey couldn't imagine she wasn't.

"I am. But it doesn't matter what I paint, I always see the things I could have done better. There are little flaws here and there."

There wasn't one thing about the painting that Lindsey could see that was a *flaw*.

"Would you like something to drink?" Sarah asked, interrupting Lindsey's thoughts.

"Sure, that would be great." She followed Sarah back down to the kitchen, taking in various paintings and photos on the walls as they passed by them. There were a few that Lindsey surmised were Julie. Sarah looked quite a bit younger in them.

Sarah opened the refrigerator and peered in. She'd stocked up on soda and juices in anticipation of Lindsey's visit. She rattled off the choices. Lindsey chose ginger ale. Sarah scooped ice from the bin in the freezer into a glass, poured the soda, and handed it to Lindsey. And then repeated the steps for herself. "Let's sit in the living room."

Lindsey sat on the couch and set her glass on a coaster on the coffee table. Sarah settled herself in one of the chairs, an end table between them. Sarah had been so intent on showing Lindsey around she hadn't had a chance to really take her in. Her dark brown hair hung in waves just above her shoulders. Her light brown eyes lit up when she talked and seemed to almost sparkle. She was definitely pretty. Fit. Seemed intelligent. There was a charisma about her that she probably wasn't even aware of. Sarah guessed she had no problem making friends or drawing people in. "Thanks so much for coming over. It was nice to find out you were so close by."

"Thanks for inviting me. Yes. I was very surprised."

"Tell me more about you. Are you from this area originally? Family? Siblings?"

Lindsey seemed to hesitate for a moment and Sarah wondered if she'd overstepped with her questions. "Whatever you're comfortable sharing," she added.

"Only child. My dad left a long time ago. My mom and I... well, let's just say it isn't the best relationship."

"Oh, I'm so sorry."

The small laugh Lindsey let out confused Sarah. "No need to be sorry. I came to grips with it a long time ago. I have great friends. *They* are my family. You know what I mean?"

Sarah's situation seemed to be the opposite. The only ones who stuck by her when she closed down were her family.

"Cricket," Lindsey continued before Sarah had a chance to answer. "Is like a sister to me. We've been best friends forever. Even work together."

"That's great. Cricket? Where did that name come from?"

This time Lindsey's laugh seemed genuine. "Her brother was three when she was born. Her parents named her Crystal. He couldn't quite say it and he was really into bugs. What three-year-old boy isn't? Anyway, he called her Cricket and it stuck." The smile that lit up her face was so appealing that Sarah found herself smiling in return.

"What about you? What is your family like?" Lindsey asked.

"My parents have been wonderful through everything. As has my sister, Mary. She's two years older than me. I can only imagine what bug name she would have given me if she couldn't pronounce my name."

"Maybe scarab beetle."

Sarah laughed. "Yuck. What is that?"

"It's a huge scary beetle probably a foot long, and get this…" Lindsey paused. "It eats people."

"What?"

"It's a well-known fact that I just made up. You can look it up on the internet, but you'll have to wait till tomorrow. I haven't posted it yet."

Sarah laughed. It felt good—and strange at the same time. It had been a long time since she truly laughed from somewhere deep inside herself. She'd almost forgotten what it felt like.

"Do you make up facts often?" Sarah asked when she got her laughter under control.

"Only when necessary. You have a great laugh by the way."

"It's been a long time since I've laughed like that."

"You should do it more often."

Maybe with Lindsey around I would, Sarah thought, then brushed the thought away. She was so out of practice being around—well, anyone except her family.

"So, you have one sister?" Lindsey asked.

"And a brother. Both are married to great people. My brother has two kids of his own. They would be…" Sarah looked up as if the answer to her silent question was on the ceiling. "Let's see… hmm. Greg would be seven and Wally would be four."

"Those are great ages. Do you see them often?"

She was embarrassed to say no, and she tilted her head and shook it.

"Do they live far away?"

"No. They live across town. I just haven't been open to seeing much of anyone since…well, for a while now."

"I can understand that."

Sarah brought her eyes to Lindsey's. "Do you really?"

She had her answer in Lindsey's eyes before she even spoke. "Yes. I do. I know what it's like to feel as if your world has fallen apart and you don't know which way to turn or what to do. I know my pain wasn't the same as yours, but it still hurt."

"Did you see it coming? Did Tina give you any indication that there was trouble in paradise?"

Lindsey shook her head and Sarah saw a flash of pain cross her face. It disappeared as quickly as it had appeared. "No. I thought everything was fine. I was happy. I thought she was too. It kills me to think I couldn't see it."

"I think that sudden pain—the surprise of it—hurts the most."

"I agree."

"As you could probably tell from my emails to Julie, I have decided to get on with my life. Not that my grieving is over. I know it will rear its head again. But I'm letting it shift. I'm choosing to remember my love for Julie instead of remembering my loss."

"That is a great way to look at it."

"It isn't always easy, but I'm doing my best."

"That's all anyone could ask," Lindsey said.

"And what about you?"

Lindsey looked confused. "Me?"

"How are you dealing with the loss of Tina?" Sarah took a sip of her soda and set it down on the end table. Her hand had gotten cold from holding it, without her realizing it. She'd been so wrapped up in their conversation.

"At first, I was so hurt, and then angry. I felt like running her over with my car." She put her hands up in front of her. "Not that I would ever do it."

"I didn't think you would," Sarah said.

"After a while, I forgave her. It wasn't easy and I had to consciously decide to do it. It would have been nice if she had given me some warning that the relationship wasn't working for her and maybe a chance to try to fix it. But I realized that if she wasn't happy, she had every right to leave."

"That's very adult of you."

Lindsey laughed. "Don't let that get around. The last thing I want to be thought of is an adult."

Sarah laughed again. She found herself really enjoying Lindsey's company. This was what she really needed. Another human around her that she liked.

"Don't get me wrong. I still have moments, but for the most part I'm over it."

"Good. I'm glad."

"I'm glad you're getting on with your life, too."

"Thanks. I appreciate that. Like you said, there are moments that are hard. But I get through them and find myself on the other side of it."

"Sometimes all we can do is take it one moment at a time," Lindsey said.

"Ain't that the truth." Sarah raised her glass of soda to Lindsey. "I'll drink to that." She took another sip.

Lindsey lifted her glass in response. "Me too."

"Would you like to stay for dinner?" Sarah hoped Lindsey said yes. She couldn't remember the last time she'd cooked dinner for someone besides herself.

"I don't want you to go to any trouble."

"It's no trouble. You would actually be helping me out if you said yes. Otherwise, I'm going to be eating a bowl of cereal. And I know you wouldn't want me doing that."

"Wow. No. I'll stay if it means you'll be eating real food. You also have to let me help. I'm really good at chopping and dicing."

"Deal. Do you like steak, chicken—wait. You aren't a vegan, are you? I mean, no judgment. I should have probably asked before I started listing meat."

"Nope. Not a vegan. And steak or chicken would be fine."

"Okay. Good. Steak it is then. We can grill it..." Sarah paused. "If there's any gas left in the tank. I haven't used it in a while. Last time I tried, the cereal just kept falling through the grates."

"You eat cereal a lot, huh?" Lindsey said with a smile—such a warm, pretty smile.

"Way more than I should. But having company and real food will be a welcomed change." Sarah knew she didn't have any fresh vegetables but was pretty sure she had a frozen bag or two. She used to be good at improvising meals when Julie was working late. She would have gone shopping if she'd had any idea she'd be inviting Lindsey to stay for dinner. Oh well, they'd figure it out. "Or we can order a pizza," she said. That would solve the problem of trying to scrounge for food, and she wouldn't have to worry about defrosting the steak.

"Let's do that. Quick, easy, less cleanup."

"I like the way you think," Sarah said.

"Thanks. It's just something my brain does."

"I've heard that's a possibility." Sarah pulled her phone out of her pocket and opened the app to order pizza. She'd used it way too often the last couple of years. But she supposed it was better than a bowl of Cheerios. "What do you like on your pizza?"

Lindsey gave her several suggestions and the pizza was delivered in record time.

"This is really good." Lindsey swiped at her chin to catch a drop of sauce that had escaped. "Thanks so much for this. I really appreciate it."

"I appreciate the company," Sarah replied. She was so glad to have Lindsey there. "Maybe we can take in a movie sometime. If that's something you would be interested in." She didn't want to seem pushy or worse yet, desperate.

"I would like that."

"Great. Why don't you check it out, pick one, and let me know. Any movie except that one with Whoopi Goldberg. I saw that one with my sister. Does next Friday evening or Saturday work for you?"

Lindsey did a quick check on her phone calendar. She had plans with Cricket on Friday night. They usually had a girls' night out once a month. Plenty of drinks and an Uber ride home, usually to Lindsey's where Cricket would spend the night and take plenty of Advil in the morning. "Saturday works. I'll put it in. Would you prefer an evening showing or a matinee?"

"How about matinee and maybe we can figure out something to do afterward."

"That sounds like a plan."

"Wonderful." Sarah couldn't remember the last time she'd done anything with a friend. At least she hoped she could count Lindsey as a friend.

"I should get going," Lindsey said. She carried her paper plate and napkin into the kitchen and tossed them in the trash can. Sarah walked her to the door. "Thank you so much for coming. I've really enjoyed meeting you."

"Me too." Lindsey gave her a quick hug.

Sarah leaned against the doorjamb as she watched Lindsey walk to her car. She gave a little wave as Lindsey backed out onto the street. The night air had turned chilly, and she wrapped her arms around herself. Talking with Lindsey made Sarah realize just how shut away from the world she had been. She found her phone on the end table where she left it after ordering the pizza and called her brother.

Thomas answered on the second ring. "Sarah?" he said as if he expected it to be someone else.

"Yep. It's me. Sarah. Your long-lost sister."

"Everything all right?"

Sarah shook her head. His question—the same one her sister had asked her—was further proof of just how absent she'd been. "I am. I'm calling to invite you, Robin, and the kids over for…" For what? She hadn't gotten that far in her head before she called him. "Umm, for a movie night. We can put something on for the kids while the adults chat. Popcorn. Wine."

"We don't let the kids drink wine anymore. Not since that drunken incident with Wally and the police."

"Wally and the police?" Sarah said, confused until she realized Thomas was joking. "No wine for the kids then. Does apple juice cause problems with the law?"

"Apple juice is fine. We would love to see you."

"Friday evening?"

"Let me double-check with Robin, but that should be fine. What would you like us to bring?"

Sarah didn't know too many men who would have asked that question. Her brother had always been that thoughtful kind of guy and she was glad to see that hadn't changed. "Just your beautiful selves. It's been far too long, and that's my fault. Thomas, I'm sorry about that."

"Sarah, don't sweat it. I know you've been through a lot. I'm just glad for the invite." They worked out the details and Sarah hung up, happy she'd made the call. It had been long overdue.

She wouldn't have blamed him if he was mad at her for not being more in touch. She was so lucky to have the family she had. She thought back to what Lindsey had said about her family or lack of it. She wondered what kind of friends they would turn out to be. Close friends she hoped. The thought of that was appealing. Very appealing.

❖

Back at home, Lindsey was restless. That was so unlike her. She'd had a really nice time. She liked Sarah. A lot. More than she thought was a good idea.

Cricket was probably still on her date with the doctor. Trevor. Of course, his name was Trevor. What else would a doctor handsome enough to be on the cover of magazines be called.

She had other friends, of course, but didn't feel like calling any of them. She unloaded the dishwater, refreshed Maximus's water, and added a little more food to his bowl. He rubbed his body against her legs as his way of saying thanks.

"You're welcome, guy."

How strange life was sometimes. Who would have ever thought she would make a friend because of an error in an email address? And she did hope she could count Sarah as a friend. If today was any indication, they were destined to be *good* friends.

Sarah had been so easy to talk to. There were no uncomfortable gaps as there could be when meeting someone new. Her phone pinged, interrupting her thoughts.

It was from Sarah. *Thank you so much for a lovely day.*

Yeah, she liked Sarah. This was just one more reason why. She was so kind. Thoughtful. The kind of person Lindsey was happy to add to her life.

I had a very nice time as well and look forward to that movie and seeing you again. Lindsey typed and then deleted it. She retyped, *I had a very nice time, too.* This time she hit send. She got a smiley face emoji in return.

Why was she hesitant to show just how much she enjoyed Sarah's company or how much she was looking forward to seeing her again? "Because I don't want to scare her away," she said to Maximus.

He looked up at her and purred his response.

"I see you agree. I haven't felt this way about anyone since Tina walked out on us."

Maximus walked out of the room, showing his obvious disdain for what Tina had done to them.

"I agree," Lindsey called after him. She scooped some ice cream into a bowl and settled down with it in front of the TV. Maximus jumped up and lay down next to her, watching every move she made with the spoon. "You are not getting any," she told him. She'd made the mistake of letting him lick the bowl once. As much as he enjoyed it, it didn't sit well in his stomach, and it showed in the extra stinky litter box. "We aren't doing that again."

She flipped though the channels and settled on an old romcom with Tom Hanks. One nice thing about Tina leaving was that Lindsey got to watch whatever she wanted. Tina hated rom-coms. *Too predictable* she'd say. *Not realistic.* Of course, it wasn't realistic. That was the whole point—let go of reality and live in a perfect fantasy world for a while. She wondered how Sarah felt about romantic movies. Probably hard for her to watch since losing Julie. That wasn't the case for her when Tina left. Lindsey watched more rom-coms in the first two months than she'd watched in the whole time they'd been together. It was her way of telling Tina she could go to hell.

She pushed any thoughts of Tina from her mind and replaced them with thoughts of Sarah. Yes. That was better. Much better.

CHAPTER FIVE

Thomas's kids had gotten so big since the last time Sarah had seen them. She wasn't sure if they would be shy around her, but they both ran to her with hugs. She gave them both a tight squeeze.

"How are you doing? Really?" Robin asked Sarah as they waited for the microwave popcorn to finish.

"Much better. I mean..." She let the words drift off. It somehow felt disloyal to Julie to say that.

"Better is good. But I get the feeling that isn't all there is to it." She and Robin had once been close. She couldn't have asked for a better sister-in-law who turned out to be a good friend. Obviously, Robin could still see right through her.

"I really am doing better. It feels weird to say that." The microwave beeped and Sarah pulled the bag of popcorn out by the corners, careful not to burn her fingers.

"I'm sure Julie would want you to get on with your life. You aren't being disloyal to her, you know."

Sarah turned to Robin. She'd hit it right on the head. She'd forgotten how intuitive Robin could be. "That's exactly what it feels like."

"Of course. You were together for a long time. You loved her. Getting on with your life without her feels like you are lessening her importance."

"How do you do that? How do you read my mind?"

Robin laughed. She tucked a strand of her long red hair behind her ear. "Just gifted, I guess."

"You should have your own show. Robin the Great. She'll read your mind and solve your dilemmas." Sarah pulled at the corners of the popcorn bag to release the steam and poured the contents into a large bowl.

"If only," Robin said. "I can't read your brother's mind."

"Would you want to?"

Robin leaned her back against the kitchen counter and crossed her arms. "No. Probably not. God only knows what's going on in there. It could be quite frightening."

Sarah smiled. She realized she'd been doing that much more lately. It was starting to feel more natural. For some reason, the realization brought Lindsey to mind and how much she'd smiled and even laughed when they were together.

Sarah handed the bowl of popcorn to Robin and poured two cups of apple juice. Once the kids were settled down with a movie and popcorn, Sarah poured each of the adults a glass of wine.

Thomas sat between the kids on the couch, while Robin and Sarah sat off to the side so they could chat. Sarah told Robin about the email mistake and how she'd met Lindsey.

"That's quite the story," Robin said. "Seems like a friendship that was meant to be."

She did agree that the Universe must have played a hand in it. She was glad it had worked out the way it did.

They chatted about Sarah's upcoming art show, the kids, and life in general. It felt good to just be normal and spend time with family. Normal. Nothing had been normal in her life the last two years.

"What are you two chatting about over there?" Thomas asked.

"Women stuff," Robin responded.

"Like period stuff or lesbian stuff?" he asked.

Robin shook her head. "Is that what you think women stuff is?"

"What else is there?"

Robin threw a wadded napkin at him. He caught it before it hit him. "Shh," he said, putting his finger to his mouth. "This is getting good. They are going to figure out how to stop winter." He turned his attention back to the TV and Robin turned her attention back to Sarah.

"He's such a man-boy."

"I heard that," Thomas said without turning his head.

"He's a man-boy with good hearing," Robin said.

Sarah had just taken a sip of her wine and struggled to swallow it as a laugh threatened to bubble up. She covered her mouth with her hand in case some wine sneaked out. Luckily it didn't.

"I've missed you," Sarah said to Robin once the danger of spitting her wine had passed.

Robin laid her hand on top of Sarah's. "I've missed you too. We need to get together more often."

"We do," Sarah agreed. And she meant it. She needed to see her family more. And as far as her friends went, well, she needed to rethink which ones were her real friends. So many of them had abandoned her when Julie died. Granted, they probably didn't know how to act around her. But if they couldn't be there in her darkest hour, she didn't want them as she was coming back into the light. But she could figure all of that out later.

The movie was coming to an end, and she wanted to spend some time with the kids. "What did you think?" she asked them as the credits rolled.

"I loved it," Thomas said. "Especially that little snowman guy."

Sarah laughed. "I was talking to Greg and Wally."

"I loved it, too," Greg said.

"Me too," Wally added.

"What was your favorite part?" Sarah asked.

"Coming to Aunt Sarah's house," Greg said in a loud voice. Wally threw up his arms. "Mine too."

Unexpected tears welled up in Sarah's eyes and she wiped them away. "Oh, I'm so glad. That was my favorite part too. I've missed you little guys."

"We're not so little," Wally said.

"You're four," Greg said to him. "You are little."

"Am not." Wally folded his arms defiantly in front of him.

Sarah held out her arms to him. "You are both growing so big." She wrapped him in a hug. "You aren't my little man anymore."

"Can I be your big man?" he asked.

"Yes. Of course."

Wally turned to his brother. "See. I'm a big man."

"Are not."

Sarah laughed. "You're both my big men." She pointed at Greg. "And no fighting."

"We won't," he said and stuck his tongue out at his brother.

The time seemed to fly by and before she knew it they were walking out the door so the boys could go to bed at a decent hour. All in all, it had been a very nice visit and just what Sarah needed. She cleaned up the kitchen and loaded glasses and bowls into the dishwasher. It would save her from doing it in the morning. She wanted to make sure everything was clean in case Lindsey came back to her house after the movie the next day. She was looking forward to seeing her again. A lot.

❖

"All set?" Lindsey asked Cricket.

"Just waiting for my credit card," Cricket responded. As if on cue, the bartender handed Cricket the card and receipt. "All set now," she said, turning her attention back to Lindsey.

Lindsey pulled her phone from her back pocket and pulled up the Uber app. "Driver's almost here. Let's wait outside."

Cricket nodded and followed her out. The temperature had dropped considerably since they'd arrived at the bar a few hours ago. Lindsey zipped her jacket and wrapped her arms around herself. Cricket didn't seem bothered by the cold, and Lindsey assumed it may have had something to do with how much she'd drunk—at least twice as much as Lindsey had. Under normal circumstances, she would have matched Cricket drink for drink, but she wanted to be clearheaded for her date—no, it wasn't a date, it was movie with a friend—the next day.

She'd sent a text to Sarah earlier with a list of movies and times. Sarah had told her to pick something, but she didn't know Sarah well enough to know her taste so she thought she should leave the final decision to her. Sarah had responded immediately. One more thing Lindsey liked about her. She never had to wait long for a response or wonder if Sarah still wanted to get together.

Their ride pulled into the parking lot, and they climbed into the back seat. Cricket leaned her head on Lindsey's shoulder and closed her eyes. It wouldn't be the first time that she fell asleep on the ride to Lindsey's house. Lindsey knew she'd been keeping late hours with her new boyfriend.

The driver wasn't chatty, and Lindsey appreciated that. Normally she wouldn't have cared, but after a night of drinking and all the talking Cricket had done, the silence was welcomed. Not that Lindsey blamed Cricket. She was so excited about her new relationship. If Lindsey was being honest with herself—and she usually was—she was a little jealous. Not jealous of someone else taking Cricket's attention. She deserved to be happy. Jealous of two people starting on an exciting adventure together. Lindsey wished she had that too. Sarah's face drifted through her mind and she pushed the picture away. Lindsey sighed.

Cricket lifted her head and looked at her. "What?"

"What what?"

"I know you well enough to know that you have been lost in your head and that sound means you're trying to let some thought go."

Lindsey let out a small laugh. "You got all that from one little sigh?"

"I did."

The driver pulled into Lindsey's driveway. "Here you go, ladies. Have a great night."

Once inside, Cricket continued the conversation. "So? What were you thinking about?"

Lindsey took a few moments to hang their coats in the closet. It gave her time to come up with an answer. "I was thinking about how happy I am for you."

"I know I highjacked the conversation tonight talking about Trevor and I'm sorry for that."

Lindsey shook her head. "No. No. It's fine. I'm glad it's going so well."

"There's something else on your mind." Cricket tapped Lindsey on the shoulder. "I kind of felt it all night but didn't want to say anything. I figured if you wanted to tell me, you would. But you haven't. So now I'm asking."

That was the Cricket Lindsey knew and loved. Usually. Tonight, her direct questions were a little too much.

Cricket tilted her head and looked at Lindsey for several long moments. Lindsey was sure she was reading her mind. She must have read her face as well. "Never mind."

"Okay. Stop begging. I was thinking about Sarah, among other things."

"Other things?" Cricket followed Lindsey into the kitchen.

Lindsey filled two glasses with water and handed one to Cricket. "I like her, Cricket."

"And that's bad why?"

Lindsey drank half of her glass of water before answering. "I don't know. She needs a friend, not someone chasing her."

"Is that what you're doing?"

"Drink that." Lindsey pointed to the glass in Cricket's hand. "No. I'm not. And I know it sounds crazy. I mean our brief history includes some misdirected emails, texts, one phone call, and meeting once. How could I be developing feelings so soon?"

Cricket set the still full glass of water on the counter and took Lindsey's hand. "Stop beating yourself up over this. It makes perfect sense. If I played for your team, I would have developed feelings from her emails alone. They were so…" She seemed to be searching for the right words. "Tender. Thoughtful. Heartfelt." And it seemed she found them.

"I'm not being stupid?"

"You are not."

"Drink your water."

Cricket did as she was told and downed it all without stopping.

"What do I do?"

"Be her friend if that's what she needs. If an opportunity for more develops, jump on it."

"So, you're saying I should jump on her?"

Cricket swatted Lindsey's arm. "Stop. We're being serious here."

"I know. I still feel like I'm overreacting. These feelings are wrong."

"Feelings aren't right or wrong. They just *are*." Cricket shook her head. "You know how long I've liked Trevor and you didn't think my feelings were wrong."

"You had an actual chance of being together. This crush is going to lead to nowhere."

"You don't know that."

Lindsey downed the rest of her water. She hadn't had that much to drink but wanted to avoid the risk of dehydration anyway. She was nothing if not responsible. She was tiring of this conversation. The topic was moot. It didn't matter what her feelings were or what Cricket thought of them. The reality was what it was, and no amount of dreaming or wishing was going to change that.

❖

Sarah read the text from Lindsey. *Would you like me to pick you up or meet you at the theater?*

She hadn't even considered that option, but it would be nice to spend the extra time with her. *Riding together would be great.*

Excellent. Movie starts at noon. How about I pick you up at 11:30?

Absolutely! Sarah responded.

See you soon.

Sarah sent a thumb's up and smiley face emoji back.

She was dressed and ready when Lindsey arrived. She grabbed a jacket even though the day proved to be warm. She had no idea how long they would be out and didn't want to risk a chilly evening. The older she got the more the cold affected her. At the age of forty—how the hell did that happen—she worried that she would need a parka by the time she was fifty.

"Hi there. Come on in."

"Thanks." Lindsey looked cute—very cute—in her dark gray slacks and deep maroon shirt that dipped just enough to reveal a bit of cleavage. A gold chain lay against her silky-smooth skin.

Sarah brought her eyes up from Lindsey's décolletage—was that the right word—up to her eyes, hoping Lindsey didn't notice what had caught Sarah's attention. The fact that it had took Sarah by surprise. She couldn't remember the last time she noticed anything about another woman. She wasn't sure how she felt about that. If the reaction from her body was any indication, she liked it. It also made her feel guilty. She pushed both feelings away and smiled at Lindsey, hoping it looked genuine and not forced. The smile Lindsey returned told her she had succeeded.

"You look nice," Lindsey said.

"Thank you. You do too." Sarah prayed that the heat that rose up her neck didn't result in her blushing. What the hell? "Excuse me. Be right back." She made her way to the bathroom and peered at herself in the mirror. Her cheeks were rosy red but not as bad as she'd expected them to be. She briefly considered splashing cold water on her face but thought it might mess up the little bit of makeup she'd applied.

She waited a few minutes for the color to leave her cheeks before rejoining Lindsey, who was still standing by the door. "Oh my God. I'm so sorry. I want you to make yourself at home while you're here. You could have sat down and made yourself comfortable."

"I didn't want to overstep," Lindsey replied. She shrugged.

"Don't be silly. Please, don't stand on formalities here."

"Noted. We should probably get going if you're ready."

"I am."

Sarah studied Lindsey's profile as Lindsey kept her eyes on the road. She certainly was pretty. Tiny lines around her eyes deepened when she smiled. Which she seemed to do often. "How old are you?" Sarah asked, surprising herself. She hadn't been quite able to figure it out.

"I thought there was a rule about asking a woman her age," Lindsey responded, looking at her. There was that smile again.

"I figured by now we must be friends."

"We are."

"And as your friend, I can't help wondering. I mean you look great. If you're sixty that would be amazing. But if you're twenty—well—I guess that would mean you've had a hard life." She added a laugh to let Lindsey know she was joking.

"How old do you think I am?"

"Oh no. I'm not playing that game. That would only get me in trouble."

"Why? Would your guess insult me?"

"Thirty-five."

"Ooh. You're brave."

"You told me to guess."

"Do you always do what you're told?" Another smile.

"I refuse to answer that. Sooo…" She drew the word out. "How old are you?"

"You're very close. I'm thirty-eight. You?"

"Me what?"

"Turnabout is fair play. How old are you? And don't tell me to guess. I'm not as brave as you are."

Sarah shook her head. "That's not fair."

"Life's not fair." Lindsey paused. "I hate that saying by the way. I don't know why I use it. It was my mother's favorite line."

"I'm sorry."

"No need to be sorry. It's not my life anymore. I have to admit that I cringe when I hear my mother's words coming out of my mouth."

"Why do you do it? Repeat things she'd said, I mean."

Lindsey seemed to think about it for a few long moments and Sarah wondered if she shouldn't have asked the question.

"I've never thought about that before. I guess because she pounded some stuff in my head as I was growing up and some of it comes leaking out when I talk." She stopped at a traffic light and turned her attention to Sarah. "I hate leaking by the way."

Sarah burst out laughing. "Do you leak often?"

"Not if I can help it. You?"

"Same."

"Age?"

"Are we back to that?"

The light turned green, and Lindsey continued to drive. "We are, because you didn't answer."

"Turned forty last month."

"You're holding up pretty good for an old lady."

"Hey. I'm only two years older than you."

"Yes, and in two years I'll be an old lady too."

"Forty is the new twenty. Or is it the new black? I always get those things confused."

Lindsey turned into the huge parking lot for the theater. "I think orange is the new black, so forty must be the new twenty."

At least a dozen current movie posters lined the walls as they entered the building with several more that said COMING SOON. Lindsey paid for two tickets despite Sarah's objections.

They passed on popcorn and made their way to theater number five. Lindsey opened the door and motioned for Sarah to go in first. It took Sarah a few moments for her eyes to adjust to the dim lighting. Just as she did the room went black, except for the tiny lights along the floor. It wasn't enough to see clearly, and Sarah stopped. Lindsey apparently hadn't noticed and ran right into her. In an obvious attempt to stop her forward motion, Lindsey's hands brushed Sarah's rear end before coming to rest on her waist, holding on to her.

Sarah closed her eyes and swallowed. The feeling of someone else's—Lindsey's hands—on her felt—she wasn't sure. Good. Strange. Guilt provoking. Good.

"I'm so sorry," Lindsey whispered, so close to her ear that it sent shivers down Sarah's spine.

Sarah let out a breath. "It's okay." The room lit up as the previews started and Sarah continued down the aisle to the middle seats. "How's this?" She realized that Lindsey's hands were still on her waist.

"Perfect," Lindsey said, dropping her hands.

The warmth they'd created went cold and Sarah missed the feeling. It seemed that it was more than just her waist that heated up.

Shit, Lindsey thought. Her hands had actually brushed against Sarah's butt before she'd gotten control of them and grabbed Sarah around the waist. Neither move was very smart. She hoped Sarah didn't think less of her. *It was good for me. Was it good for you?* She told her brain to shut up. *Not funny. Well, a little funny.* She suppressed the giggle that rose up her throat at the thought. She covered it with a cough.

She settled down in the seat next to Sarah and glanced at her. Sarah seemed wrapped up in the preview that was playing on the screen. Or was she pretending to watch to avoid looking at Lindsey after that embarrassing exchange? Lindsey wasn't sure. She followed Sarah's lead and put her attention on the screen.

The images flashed before her eyes without her absorbing what she was seeing. Her thoughts went again and again to the woman who was sitting beside her and how great it felt to touch her, even if it wasn't intentional. Was it something about Sarah or had she just been lonely and Sarah just happened to be around? No. That definitely wasn't it. She'd gone out on a few dates since Tina left, but she hadn't felt this way about any of those women. She'd given up on the idea of dating or meeting anyone special. There was no one at work that interested her. She was pretty sure she was the only lesbian in the small company. And the dating sites proved to be more frustrating than fruitful. She'd never realized how many crazy women there were.

"That one looks good," Sarah whispered.

Lindsey focused on the screen just in time to see the words *Coming in August*. She had no idea what movie it was. "We'll have to check it out," she said, hoping Sarah was still in her life by then. She couldn't see a reason why she wouldn't be—as long as she learned to keep her hands to herself. No more booty brushing or waist grabbing.

Five more previews and three commercials later, the movie started. Lindsey had to keep reminding herself to pay attention. It wasn't that the movie was boring. It was that her brain—and apparently her libido—were more interested in how her arm brushed against Sarah's or how Sarah laughed. It was a beautiful sound, and it went straight to Lindsey's heart.

"That was good," Sarah said as the credits rolled. "Did you like it?"

"I did."

"Thanks for suggesting it. It's just what I needed."

"You picked it out," Lindsey reminded her.

"Yeah, from your short list. I need to get out more. I didn't recognize most of the stars in those upcoming movies."

"I'll take you out more," Lindsey volunteered. "Today, a movie. Tomorrow, Paris. Or would you prefer Hawaii?"

"Hmm." Sarah tapped her chin. "Let's do both?"

"You got it. I better start working overtime and maybe get a second job. So I can afford to show you the world."

"You don't have to show me the world. You just need to be my friend."

Friend. Just friends. "I can do that. It would be much cheaper."

"Are you calling me a cheap date?"

Date? Now that sounded much better, although Lindsey was sure Sarah didn't mean it like that. "Not at all. You are a not too expensive date."

"That's so much better."

"Isn't it though?"

"I've always wanted to see the Louvre. So maybe you *should* check out a second job." The lights came back up as the credits ended and Lindsey could see Sarah's smile. She would happily take a second job to take Sarah to France to see that smile.

"The Louvre? That's a museum, right?"

"Correct. That's where the *Mona Lisa* is. And *Venus de Milo*."

"That's the chick with no arms?"

Sarah laughed again. "Yes. I can see you are obviously an art expert."

"I believe I would be called an art aficionado. But I don't get why they would make a statue with no arms."

"I'm sure she had arms once. But she's over two thousand years old. If you were that old you probably wouldn't have arms either."

"Excellent point. The Louvre. Got it. Saving for the trip starting now."

"I wouldn't make you take me to the Louvre if you're not interested in art. I can go by myself. You can wait for me at that little café down the street."

"So, you've been there before?"

"I have not."

"Then how do you know there's a little café down the street?"

"It's Paris. There are probably little cafés down every street."

Lindsey watched as a teenage boy started going through the seats with a garbage bag collecting trash. She had been so engrossed in the conversation that she hadn't realized the room had cleared out and they were the only ones left. "Should we go look for a little café down the street now? A late lunch maybe?"

"Excellent idea. I know just the place."

They were there in no time and were seated immediately, seeing they had missed the lunch rush.

"Drinks?" The waitress, Betsy her name tag said, laid two menus on the table. She didn't seem to be having a good day.

"I would love a glass of water," Sarah said.

"Make that two," Lindsey added.

"Yep. Back in a few minutes to get your orders." She disappeared without another word.

"She seems nice," Lindsey said with a straight face.

Sarah laughed. "I noticed."

She loved that laugh and Lindsey made a mental note to make her laugh as much as possible.

The waitress returned with their waters and her *less than friendly* personality. "What can I get you?"

They hadn't even had a chance to look at their menus. "Can we get a few more minutes? Please?" Lindsey gave her one of her best smiles, hoping to brighten her day. Maybe. Betsy turned and walked away.

Sarah picked up the menus and handed one to Lindsey. "We better figure out what we want before we get in trouble." She nodded in the direction of the waitress.

"We wouldn't want that. I'm going to get that woman to smile before our lunch is over," Lindsey said.

"How are you going to do that?"

"No idea. But I believe in good ripples."

"What are good ripples?" Sarah asked.

Lindsey sipped her water before answering. "Ripples are what we all put out in the world. Our lovely waitress is putting out very negative ripples today. When I was in my twenties I worked with the elderly as a home aide. One of my clients, Don, had just turned eighty when I started working with him. He had been fighting some major medical problems for years and said to me one time that he thought he was just taking up space on this earth."

"Wow," Sarah said. "That's an awful way to feel."

"It is," Lindsey continued. "But the thing is he thought because he was so frail that he was useless. But nothing was further from the truth. There was never a time when I left his house that he didn't thank me and tell me how much he appreciated what I did for him. There was never a time when he didn't thank the cashier at Wegmans for her..." Lindsey did air quotes. "Fine service."

"He sounds like a hell of a guy," Sarah said.

"He was for sure. Don's ripples were always so kind and gentle. They reached far and wide and continued to vibrate out into the world even after he died. He taught me a lot. I was so happy I had gotten the chance to get to know him."

"That's a great story," Sarah said. "Thank you for sharing it with me. It sounds like Don was lucky to have you in his life as well. I've never thought about that before. Ripples. I like it." And she found she liked Lindsey even more after that story. Lindsey had said she found her family in her friends. It sounded like she also found her family with Don.

They were ready when Betsy returned, order pad in hand.

"I love your hair," Lindsey said to her.

"Thanks," the waitress said. No smile.

"Do you style it yourself? The color is beautiful."

One side of her mouth went up. Not a full smile but not the grumpy face she'd had a moment before. "Yeah. Just blow-dry it. Nothing special."

"Well, it frames your face beautifully." Lindsey grinned at her.

Sarah took in the exchange with interest. There it was. A smile spread across the waitress's face. "Thanks," she said. "Are you ready to order?"

"We are," Lindsey said. "And we appreciate your patience."

Betsy smiled again. "Of course. What can I get for you?"

They gave her their orders and off she went.

"That was impressive," Sarah said, once Betsy walked away.

"It was all true. She has beautiful hair. You just find something nice about someone and mention it."

"Ripples," Sarah said.

"Ripples."

"Would you like to come in?" Sarah asked Lindsey as they pulled into her driveway.

"Sure, for a little while."

"Great," Sarah said, and she meant it. She was having a very good day, and she wasn't ready for it to end.

"Wine?" she asked once they were inside. She hung her jacket up in the entryway closet.

"Yes. That would be good."

"Sit. Get comfortable. I'll be right back."

Sarah returned balancing two glasses, a bottle of white wine, and a corkscrew. Lindsey stood and took a few steps to her, taking the bottle and corkscrew.

"Thanks," Sarah said.

"Should I open this?" Lindsey asked.

"Yes. Unless you know of another way to get the wine out." Sarah set the glasses on the coffee table.

"Smart-ass." Lindsey opened the bottle with ease and poured wine into the glasses.

Sarah held up her glass and waited until Lindsey did the same. "Here's to new friends and misdirected emails." She clinked her glass to Lindsey's.

"I'll drink to that. Then again, I'll drink to anything."

Sarah managed to swallow the sip of wine she had in her mouth. "Stop. You're going to make me choke."

"Don't worry. I know mouth-to-mouth. I was a Boy Scout for eight years." Lindsey paused and scrunched up her face. "Or was it Girl Scouts? I get those two mixed up." Lindsey sat.

Sarah sat next to her. "Were the other scouts girls or boys?"

Lindsey appeared to think for a few seconds. "Girls I think."

"Then it was Girl Scouts."

Lindsey opened her mouth wide, and she shook her head. "Wow. I hadn't thought of it that way."

"By the way, I don't think mouth-to-mouth is done for choking. At least not for the first step."

"It is if you're choking on wine. You need to suck the wine out of the victim's throat."

"Oh. Good to know."

"On a serious note," Lindsey said. "I had a really nice day."

Sarah's heart warmed. "Me too. Thank you for that. We need to do this again. Soon." Very soon.

CHAPTER SIX

H i, Mom." Sarah said into her phone. She scooped another tablespoon of ground coffee into the coffee maker and pressed the start button. She cleared her throat to dislodge the last bits of sleep making her voice sound rough.

"Thomas and Mary are coming for Sunday dinner with their families today. It would be great if you could join us." Her mother had invited her every Sunday since forever. She and Julie often accepted the invitation, but Sarah had rarely gone since losing Julie. She appreciated the fact that her mother still invited her.

"Sure, Mom. I'll come. What would you like me to bring?"

There were several seconds of silence.

"Mom?"

"Yes. You're coming? That's wonderful. Your father will be so happy. Me too."

Sarah took a clean mug from the dishwasher and poured French vanilla creamer in, barely covering the bottom of the cup.

"Dinner is at three o'clock, but feel free to come over earlier," her mother said. Dinner was always at three on Sundays.

"Okay. Would you like me to bring anything?" Sarah repeated.

"Nope. Just you. See you in a little while. Love you."

"Love you, too. Bye."

Sarah pressed the end button on her phone and set it on the counter. She pulled the quarter-full coffee pot out and watched two drips of coffee drop onto the warming plate and sizzle. After pouring herself a cup, she replaced the pot so it could finish brewing.

The rolled-up newspaper that she retrieved from the front steps was slightly damp. She rarely read it anymore. It was Julie who had wanted a subscription to the Sunday paper and Sarah had never bothered canceling it. She skipped over the bad news and focused on the uplifting human interest stories. She read the comic page even though she rarely found it funny.

She refolded the paper and tossed it in the recycling bin by the back door and poured herself another cup of coffee. She heard her phone ringing but wasn't sure where she'd left it. She followed the sound, coffee cup in hand, into the living room. She found her phone under the coupon section of the newspaper on the coffee table.

"Hello," she said without looking at the caller ID.

"Hi."

She recognized the voice right away. "Hi, Lindsey. How are you?"

"Great. I wanted to call and say thanks for a nice day yesterday."

"I enjoyed it too. There's no need to thank me."

"What are you up to today? I know it's last-minute but there's a play tonight. My friend is playing piano in the pit. I was wondering if you would like to go."

"Playing piano in the pit? What does that mean?"

"The orchestra pit. It's a musical."

She hadn't been to a play in years. "I love musicals. What time is it? I'm going to my parents' for dinner at three."

"It starts at eight."

"That works. Would you like to come to dinner at my parents' with me?"

"Meet your parents already? This is getting serious really fast." Lindsey laughed.

Sarah laughed along with her. "Too fast? If you don't want to meet them, you can stay in the car, and I'll bring food out to you."

"You would do that for me?"

"Of course." Sarah liked her a lot. There was probably a lot of things she would do for her.

"You're very kind. I would feel bad making you do that. If you're serious and your mom wouldn't mind another person at the table, I would be happy to join you."

"She won't mind. Growing up we always had a stray or two join us for Sunday dinner or holidays."

"So, you think of me as a stray?" Lindsey snickered. "Nice."

"You know that's not what I meant." Sarah hurried to explain. "Friends who didn't have—"

Lindsey cut her off. "I'm teasing. I know what you meant. And to be honest, growing up I was one of those strays, often eating at friends' houses to avoid my mother."

"That must have been so hard to grow up that way."

"It wasn't easy, but I had wonderful friends. Cricket's mom treated me like her daughter. She filled in the gaps. And she made the greatest meatloaf. And I had my grandmother. She was the best," Lindsey said. "So, yes. This stray would love to join your family for dinner."

"Excellent."

They chatted for ten more minutes. Lindsey was so easy to talk to. It never felt awkward, even when there was a moment or two of silence.

Sarah took advantage of the time she had before dinner and worked on her newest painting. She was pleased with her progress. She hadn't struggled with it, like she had with the first one. Maybe it *was* like riding a bike. Once she was on it and pedaled a few times, her muscle memory took over and she rode like an expert.

She considered the painting done by the time she cleaned her brushes two hours later. A quick glance at the clock told her she had enough time to sketch out the next painting. She printed out her reference photo, grabbed a sixteen-by-twenty canvas and sat at her desk. "Alexa, set an alarm for two o'clock." The last thing she needed was to lose track of time—which was easy to do when she was immersed in her creativity.

She finished the drawing before her alarm went off, sprayed it with fixative so the pencil lines wouldn't smudge when she applied paint, and changed her clothes. After applying a thin layer of makeup, she made her way downstairs to wait for Lindsey. She didn't have to wait long.

"Hey, stranger," Sarah said. "Come on in." She stepped back so Lindsey could scoot by her.

"It's stranger now? Earlier it was stray. What's next?"

"Coffee?"

"Now you're calling me coffee?"

"I am not. I'm calling you Lindsey. So, Lindsey, would you like a cup of coffee?"

"I would. Thank you, scarab beetle."

"Hey. Hey."

"Are you trying to sing that Hank Williams song? 'Hey, Good Lookin'.'" Lindsey followed Sarah into the kitchen.

"I've never heard of that song. I have heard of Hank Williams Junior but don't know what he sings." Sarah grabbed a cup from the cupboard and poured the last of the coffee into it. "Creamer, sugar, milk?"

"Creamer, please. This would be Hank Williams Senior, and my grandmother played his records all the time."

"You mentioned your grandmother before. Were you close?" Sarah handed the creamer to Lindsey.

"I spent a lot of time with her as a kid. She died when I was ten. It was hard. She was like my second mother." She paused. "Or like my first mother. I'm trying to root figs, sort of like a tribute to her."

"Figs? Like in Fig Newtons?"

Lindsey laughed. "Sort of. You've never had fresh figs?"

"I didn't even know there were fresh figs. What does rooting them mean?"

"You take a fig cutting—a piece of a branch from a tree. Like six or eight inches long, and basically you put it in some sort of growing medium and hope it grows roots."

"That's amazing. I had no idea. But why are you trying to root them? Wouldn't it be easier to just buy a tree?"

"My grandmother had a fig tree in her backyard. I would help her pick them and would eat some right from the tree. The cuttings—branches—that I am using are from *her* tree. I stopped at the house about a month ago and asked the current owners if I could take a few branches. They were kind enough to say yes."

"What a wonderful memory."

"It is. My grandmother was the best. She was always there for me."

"I'm so sorry. I know how hard loss is."

Lindsey set her cup on the counter and pulled Sarah into a hug. "I know you do. And I'm sorry for what you've been through."

Sarah hadn't expected the sudden hug and was surprised by her body's reaction to it. Warm, crossing over into hot. Comforting and comfortable. Tingling. Yes. That was what she felt. Tingly all over. It felt strange, like a long-lost memory. Kind of cob-webby and misty. It also felt scary. Like it was something she shouldn't be feeling but couldn't push away. She was relieved and yet left empty feeling when Lindsey released her.

Confused. That about summed it up. Confused by the feelings. Confused by—by what? By the guilt, her brain screamed. Her body betrayed Julie. How could she feel what she was feeling when she still loved Julie?

"Hey," Lindsey said, dipping her head to look into Sarah's eyes. "What? What are you thinking?"

"Why?" Sarah did her best to smile, but she couldn't quite pull it off.

"I know we haven't known each other long, but I can tell something just happened."

Sarah didn't know how to put into words all the strange sensations coursing through her body and mind. She didn't want Lindsey to know what feelings that hug had stirred in her. "It's nothing. We were talking about loss and it just..." She let the words trail off. "Grab your coffee and let's sit in the living room."

Lindsey must have gotten the message because she dropped the subject.

Sarah sat in one of the chairs, giving herself physical distance from Lindsey who sat on the couch. "So, your grandmother liked old music?"

Lindsey laughed and Sarah tried to ignore the way it made her heart swell. "It wasn't old when she listened to it. That song is about as country as a song can get. Do you like country music?"

"Sure. Country. Pop. Soft rock. Not so crazy about classical." She turned toward the Amazon Echo on the end table across from her. "Alexa, play 'Hey, Good Lookin'" by Hank Williams."

Alexa responded and the song played. Sarah watched Lindsey's face and could almost see her traveling back in time to her grandmother's house.

"Thank you," Lindsey said when the song ended. "I haven't heard that in years. It brings back good memories."

That was the thing about songs. They could stir up good memories or bring you down when those memories reminded you of what you lost. There were a handful of songs that Sarah couldn't listen to without crying.

"I'm glad," Sarah responded. "Glad for your good memories." She had plenty of those herself. Sometimes they were what kept her going and sometimes they crushed her very soul. It was hard when you knew you would never be making memories with your love again. She pushed the thought out of her mind. "Tell me about her. Your grandmother."

"Well," Lindsey started. "She was older than me."

"Do tell." Sarah couldn't help but smile.

"And so much wiser. I was a just a kid, but she treated me like I mattered. You know? Some people act like kids don't have feelings or that their feelings aren't important. Not to mention any names." She lowered her voice. "My mother." She cleared her throat and continued. "Anyway, her parents came over from Italy. Sicily actually. The tough part of Italy." Lindsey smiled. "I never knew her parents, but she talked about them so much I felt like I did. They were strong. Fearless. I mean you have to be to come to a different country and leave your family and friends behind. I think that shaped my grandmother. She was brave. Went skydiving when she was in her sixties. Like she jumped out of a perfectly good plane just for fun."

"Wow. She sounds amazing."

"She was. She's been gone, what, like twenty-eight years and sometimes I still miss her."

"Of course. She was an important part of your life." Lindsey did understand losing someone she loved. It somehow made Sarah feel closer to her.

"For sure."

"We should probably get going soon," Sarah said.

"Ready when you are." Lindsey finished her coffee and put the empty cup in the dishwasher.

Sarah drove the short distance to her parents' house. She let herself in the front door. Her dad always kept it locked except when he knew his kids were coming over. "Anyone home?"

Her mom came out of the kitchen wiping her hands on a dish towel. She always seemed to be doing that. "Hi, honey. I'm so glad you came." She gave Sarah a tight hug and Sarah breathed in her familiar perfume, mixed with the smell of roast beef.

"Mom, this is Lindsey. Lindsey, my mom, Judy Osborn."

Lindsey offered her hand. "So nice to meet you, Mrs. Osborn."

"We hug around here, and call me Judy." She put her arms out and waited for Lindsey to step into them. She gave her a quick hug.

"I should have warned you that we are huggers," Sarah said.

"I like it," Lindsey said.

"I hear we're huggers," her dad said as he entered the room. "Sarah." He wrapped his big bear arms around her. His rough beard brushed against her cheek. "Hi," he said to Lindsey. "I'm Dan, Sarah's dad." He held his hand out and Lindsey shook it.

"So nice to meet you. I hope it's okay that I showed up without an invitation," Lindsey said, looking from Sarah's dad to her mom.

"Don't be silly," Sarah's mother said. "Any friend of Sarah's is welcome here." She winked at Sarah. Her mother didn't wink. What was that all about? Did she think Lindsey was more than a friend? She'd have to make sure to clear that up when she got a minute alone with her.

"I appreciate that," Lindsey said.

Thomas and his family arrived a few minutes later. Sarah did the introductions.

"So nice to meet you," Robin said. "Sarah's told me about you and how you two met. What are the odds?"

Lindsey remembered what Cricket had said. "One in three hundred and thirty-five."

"For real?" Robin asked.

"Or is that one of the facts that you made up?" Sarah turned to Robin. "Lindsey makes up the most interesting facts."

Lindsey laughed. "That's what my friend Cricket said."

"And how did she come to that conclusion?" Sarah asked.

"Area codes."

"Huh?"

"Cricket looked up how many area codes there are in the U.S. Three hundred and thirty-five. So, the odds of us being in the same area code is one in three hundred and thirty-five."

"Aww, interesting," Robin said.

"I never thought of that," Sarah added.

"Aunt Sarah, will you play a game with me?" Greg tugged on her shirt.

Sarah squatted down on one knee. "Can my friend Lindsey play too?"

"Sure."

To Lindsey's surprise, the little boy took her hand and led her to the living room, followed closely by Sarah.

There was a stack of games on the bottom shelf of a bookcase in the corner. The room was large and boasted two recliners and a matching couch. The large TV—at least fifty inches, Lindsey guessed—was mounted on the wall.

Greg pulled a box from the stack. "How about this one?" he asked.

Sarah laughed. "I'm afraid I'm a little too old to play Twister. I would probably break my neck."

"You aren't old," Greg said. "Grandma's old."

Sarah put her finger to her lips. "Shh. Don't let her hear you say that. It might hurt her feelings."

"She's the one that told me," Greg said.

"Yeah, but she probably doesn't want us to agree with her." Sarah got down and looked through the games. "How about Chutes and Ladders?"

"Naw. That one's for babies."

"I guess we need one for people that aren't old and aren't babies," Lindsey said.

"Middle-aged it is." Sarah pulled out Mouse Trap. "How about this one?"

"I love that game," Greg said. "But no one will play with me because it takes so long to set up."

"Not if there's three of us doing it," Sarah said. "Lindsey, would you help me and Greg set this up?"

"Of course," Lindsey said. She sat on the floor cross legged next to the box and lifted the lid. She handed a couple of pieces to Greg. "Do you know how to do this?"

"Yep." He put a few pieces together.

"Sarah, are you going to help?" Lindsey asked. She handed her a few more pieces as well. They had the game put together in no time.

"Can I go first?" Greg asked.

Sarah tapped her chin. "I don't know. Lindsey is our guest. Do you think we should let her go first? Or I'm the oldest. Do you think maybe I should go first?"

Greg started to object.

Sarah interrupted him. "No, wait. You're the youngest. I think you should go first."

He giggled. "Okay."

Lindsey watched the interaction between Sarah and her nephew and couldn't help but admire how good Sarah was with him.

"Can I play? I wanna play?" Wally came running into the room.

"No," Greg said. "It's only for older kids and middle ages. Right, Aunt Sarah?"

"I'm older," Wally whined.

"Of course, you can play," Sarah said. She raised her eyebrows when Greg looked at her. He got the silent message and didn't object. "You and I can be partners."

"Yay," Wally said. "Oh yeah, Aunt Mary and Uncle Ralph are here. Grandma said to tell you. They came in the back door."

Lindsey looked at Sarah to see if they should get up to go greet Sarah's sister. Apparently, that wasn't the plan.

"Thanks," Sarah said to Wally. She handed the die to Greg. "Go ahead. Roll and let's see what you get."

He rolled a two and moved his green mouse. "Yay. I get a piece of cheese."

"Hey. Who cut the cheese?" a tall man with short brown hair and a neatly trimmed beard said as he came into the room.

"Uncle Ralph." Greg giggled and jumped up to give him a hug. "No one cut the cheese." He grabbed his cardboard cheese piece from the game and showed it to him. "It's already cut."

"Ahh. I see. And who is your nice friend here?" He motioned toward Lindsey.

"That's not my friend. It's Aunt Sarah's friend."

"Hi, Aunt Sarah's friend," Ralph said. "I'm Ralph, Sarah's brother-in-law."

"This is Lindsey," Sarah said. "My friend." She emphasized the word *friend*.

It made Lindsey cringe. "Hi, Ralph. Nice to meet you."

"You too." He roughed up the hair on Wally's head, who was sitting on Sarah's lap, as Sarah sat on the floor. "Hey there, Wally man. How are you doing?"

"Good," he squeaked out.

Sarah's sister, Mary, joined them and once again Sarah did the introductions.

They were just finishing up the first game of Mouse Trap—which Greg won—when Sarah's mother let them know dinner was ready. The two boys jumped up and ran to the table, leaving Lindsey and Sarah to put the game back in the box, which they did in record time. Sarah stood and offered a hand to Lindsey and pulled her up. She let go as soon as Lindsey was standing.

There were two empty chairs next to each other by the time they reached the dining room. Lindsey looked around at the group. Nine people in total, not counting her. And they all seemed to love each other. Better yet, they seemed to *like* each other. How lucky was Sarah to have such a great family. They sat down joining the large group.

"Greg," Sarah's mother said. "Your turn to say grace."

Sarah bowed her head and took Lindsey's hand. Mary, seated on the other side of Lindsey, did the same. Everyone around the table was holding hands with the person next to them. She was aware of how soft and warm Sarah's hand felt in hers.

"Thank you, dear God, for the food we are about to eat and for our family. Extra, extra special thanks for Aunt Sarah being here and for me winning Mouse Trap."

"Great job," Sarah's dad said. "I agree. Extra special thanks for having Sarah here. And her friend Lindsey," he added.

Sarah retrieved her hand and wiped a tear as it trickled down her cheek. "Thanks. I'm happy to be here." She turned to Lindsey, took her hand again and gave it a quick squeeze. Lindsey couldn't quite read the expression on her face.

Not only was Sarah happy to be with her family. She was happy to have Lindsey there as well. Family and friends. That's what life was about. Wasn't it? She'd put herself on a shelf for so long that it felt good—and strange—to be back in the swing of life.

She squeezed Lindsey's hand to convey how much she appreciated her and how thankful she was to have her in her life.

A full stomach later, Sarah helped Mary and her mother clear the table and load the dishwasher. The rest of the crew was in the living room. Sarah had insisted that Lindsey didn't need to help clean up and she should relax with everyone else in the living room. Lindsey seemed to fit right in, so Sarah wasn't worried that she would feel awkward without her being right there. Besides, she wanted to talk to her mother and make sure she knew Lindsey was only a friend.

"What's the story with Lindsey?" Mary asked. She never was one to mince words.

"I was wondering that too," Sarah's mother said.

"There is no story. She's a new friend. We met by accident."

"But she's so pretty," her mother said. "Does she play for your team?"

Sarah laughed. Her mother was obviously watching shows with lesbian characters. "My team?"

"You know," she said, lowering her voice. "The lesbians. That team."

"Mom," Mary said. "That's rude."

"What? Sarah knows about the lesbian team."

"Yes," Sarah said.

"Yes, you know about the lesbian team or, yes, she plays on it?" Mary asked.

"Both," Sarah said.

"Then why aren't you dating her? You would make such a cute couple," her mother said.

"We're friends. Not every lesbian in the world dates every other lesbian."

"That doesn't make sense. Is she single?"

Sarah was getting annoyed at the questions and worked to keep the irritation out of her voice. "Yes."

"And you're single," Mary said.

Sarah cringed. "I'm not ready to date." She must have said it louder than she intended because both her sister and mother were staring at her. Her mother's eyebrows went up so fast that Sarah thought they might fly off her face.

"Okay," her mother said after several long moments of silence. "I didn't mean to push. I mean, she's so nice and like I said, very pretty. I just thought…" She let the words drift off. "Never mind what I thought."

"Sorry," Mary said.

Sarah closed her eyes and took a deep breath. "It's okay. Yes, she's single and very pretty. We're just friends."

"Message received," Mary said.

They were quiet as her mother spooned some of the leftovers into smaller containers, sealed them and put them in a plastic grocery bag. "Here you go." She handed the bag to Sarah. "Food for the next couple of days for you."

"Thanks, Mom. I'm sorry if I was harsh, I'm just not—"

"It's okay," her mother interrupted. "We shouldn't have pushed."

"We love you and want you to be happy. That's all," Mary added.

"I know. Thank you for that. We're going to get going." She hugged her mother. "Thank you for dinner."

"Of course."

They said their good-byes and there were hugs all around.

"I really like your family," Lindsey said as they pulled out of the driveway.

"Yeah. They're great," Sarah said. Her mind returned to the conversation with her mother and sister. She couldn't argue with the fact that Lindsey was pretty. Beautiful in fact. But them as a couple? A cute couple her mother had said. She definitely wasn't ready for that. She wasn't sure if she ever would be.

CHAPTER SEVEN

Sarah did her best to keep track of what was going on in the play. It wasn't very interesting, and the fact that Lindsey was so close that she could feel the body heat coming off her made it even harder to pay attention. Lindsey's hand was on the armrest between them, and Sarah kept glancing down, wondering what it would be like to entwine their fingers together. Damn her mother and sister and their suggestion that she and Lindsey should be dating.

"What do you think?" Lindsey leaned toward her and whispered.

Sarah's first instinct was to lean away. She fought the instinct. It would have been hard to explain why she did that. "It's good," she answered, trying to ignore the sensations coursing through her body. "What do you think?"

"It's okay. A little slow."

Sarah hoped Lindsey wouldn't ask her anything specific, because she wouldn't have any idea how to answer. To her relief, Lindsey put her attention back on the play. Sarah did the same. She'd lost the thread of the plot but was able to figure some of it out. Lindsey was right. It was slow. Probably best that way, so Sarah could keep up.

"I'd like to say hello to my friend, if that's okay with you," Lindsey said as the cast took their final bow.

"Sure. Of course."

They let most of the audience file out before making their way to the stage where many of the cast and musicians were surrounded by family, friends, and fans. Lindsey grabbed Sarah's hand as they weaved between people, heading toward her friend. Sarah was so intent on keeping up with her in the crowd that she didn't have time to think about the sensation of Lindsey's hand in hers—until they stopped. Then she noticed how warm and soft it was. Lindsey absently ran her thumb back and forth across Sarah's skin, causing a ripple effect throughout Sarah's body. She pulled her hand out of Lindsey's and hoped she didn't notice. She didn't seem to. She was intent on talking to her friend.

"Ginger," Lindsey said loud enough to be heard above the buzz of the crowd.

The tall redhead turned around. "Lindsey, you made it." She pulled Lindsey into a hug.

"I wouldn't have missed it." Lindsey stepped back and put her arm around Sarah's waist to ease her forward. "This is my friend," she said. "Ginger, this is Sarah."

"Sarah. So nice to meet you. Hey," Ginger said to Lindsey. "A bunch of us are going across the street to Havart's Bar. Why don't you and Sarah join us?"

Sarah hoped that Lindsey said no. She had work in the morning and staying out late on a Sunday night wasn't the best idea. She wasn't as young as she used to be, besides the fact that she wasn't used to being out at all.

"I appreciate the invite," Lindsey said. "But I think we're going to pass. It's been a pretty full day."

"Understood. Understood." Ginger seemed very energized. "Did you enjoy the play?"

"The music was great," Lindsey said.

Ginger laughed. "Thanks. I know what you're saying." She winked.

Lindsey managed to answer the question to Ginger's satisfaction without lying. Sarah was impressed.

"Hey, listen. We need to get going. I just wanted to say hi. Give me a call during the week and we'll set up lunch or something," Lindsey said.

"Sounds good." Ginger hugged Lindsey again. "Nice meeting you, Sarah," she said again.

"You too."

They weaved their way back through the crowd around the stage, this time without Lindsey taking Sarah's hand. Sarah would have grabbed Lindsey's hand if she had been close enough. She'd lost a bit of the distance when someone stepped between them, and Lindsey kept walking while Sarah had to go around the person. Lindsey reached the door first, turned, and waited for Sarah to catch up.

"Okay?" Lindsey asked.

"Sure."

"I hope you're not disappointed that I didn't want to go to the bar with Ginger and the cast."

"Not at all."

They continued out the door to Lindsey's car. They were quiet on the ride home. Sarah was lost in her head. Confusing thoughts about Lindsey danced here and danced there, making her dizzy with their jazz routine. She wondered what was going on in Lindsey's head and why she was quiet as well. Sarah chalked it up to what Lindsey had said to Ginger. It *had* been a full day. It certainly was a much fuller day than Sarah was used to. A couple of years of doing pretty much nothing but working and vegging in front of the TV made flexing your social muscle tiring. It was a muscle she knew she needed to flex more often. With Lindsey's help she was determined to do just that. But she needed to sort out these feelings first.

❖

"How come you're so tired?" Cricket asked Lindsey the next day at work.

Lindsey pulled her attention from her computer. "I could ask you the same thing." She yawned.

"I didn't get much sleep," Cricket said. "I spent the night at Trevor's."

Lindsey sat up straighter. "You did? Does that mean what I think it means?"

Cricket looked around, disappeared into her own cubicle, and returned with her office chair. She pushed it next to Lindsey's and plopped down in it. Lindsey could tell by the smile on her face that it was *exactly* what she thought it was. Cricket spent the next ten minutes telling her just how wonderful her night had been. Lindsey was glad she spared the intimate details.

"Now," Cricket said. "Why are you so tired?"

"I spent the day with Sarah yesterday."

Cricket scooted her chair closer. "Whoa. Okay. Tell me."

"Don't get too excited. It wasn't like your night."

Cricket scrunched up her face. "Oh."

"We had dinner at Sarah's parents' house with her family."

"You basically just met her and went to her family's already? How was that?"

"Good." Lindsey smiled remembering the day. "Her family is very warm and welcoming. So different than what I grew up with."

"Yeah. I remember. You know I thought you didn't want your mother to meet *me* when we were younger. It took a while for me to realize it was *her* you were ashamed of."

"I'm sorry you felt that way." Lindsey never invited any of her friends over. Cricket didn't meet her mother until they were graduating from high school and Lindsey's mother acted like her shadow after the ceremony. She introduced herself to any and all of Lindsey's friends that they came in contact with. Lindsey was mortified, even though her mother was on her best behavior.

"It's okay. I understand. You had a good day then?"

"Yes. We went to Ginger's play afterward."

"Oh yeah. She invited me to that, but I already had plans with Trevor. How was it?"

Lindsey gave her opinion of the play. She hadn't been impressed.

"So, I didn't miss much. Although it would have been great to meet Sarah."

Lindsey didn't like that idea, for some reason. She wanted to keep Sarah to herself for a while. At least until her feelings for her settled down. And she had no doubt they would. That wasn't exactly true. She had a lot of doubts that her feelings for Sarah would ever change. She was scared by the prospect of them growing. Maybe out of control.

"Are we working or chatting?" Lindsey hadn't noticed Jason, the floor supervisor, come up behind Cricket.

Cricket turned around. "Chatting. I'm on a break."

"Don't make it too long," Jason said. He tapped on the side of Lindsey's cubicle wall.

"Got it," Lindsey said.

Jason moved on and she could hear him talking to Sally, three cubicles down.

"I'm glad things are working out so well for you and Trevor," Lindsey said.

A smile spread across Cricket's face. "Me too. I hope you get the same."

Lindsey shook her head. "I don't think that's in the cards for me. I thought Tina was my happily ever after, but we both know how that turned out."

"Tina was an ass. There are plenty of good women out there. Don't give up on love, Linz. Don't let Tina's shortcoming define the rest of your life."

"It's not just Tina. I've had a string of relationships that didn't work out."

"You haven't met the right person yet. That's all."

The right person. Was there a right person? She thought she'd never have feelings for anyone again after Tina left and the bad dates she'd been on since. Being around Sarah made her rethink that. She certainly liked her. Maybe more than like. Yeah.

Definitely more than like. But Sarah didn't seem to be in a space to start a new relationship. So that left her—nowhere.

"Don't give up," Cricket repeated. "If I'd given up, I never would have gone out with Trevor and look how great that's going."

"And you deserve it."

"Are you saying *you* don't deserve it?"

Lindsey had to think about that. Was that part of the story she told herself? She searched her soul after Tina left to try to figure out what she had done wrong to drive her away. She picked apart every conversation she could recall, every meal she ever cooked, every time she and Tina failed to connect intimately. In the end, she couldn't figure it out. But somewhere deep inside her, Cricket's words echoed through her. Did she feel like she didn't deserve a relationship and love? Maybe. She'd have to think about that one.

"Lindsey?"

"What?" She'd lost track of the question.

"Are you saying you don't deserve love?" Cricket repeated.

"No. I'm not saying that. I don't know what I'm saying."

"Back to work," Jason said as he went past, going back toward his office.

Lindsey turned her chair back toward her computer.

"We aren't finished," Cricket said.

"I am. I give Jason five minutes before he comes through here again to check on us." She clicked her mouse to bring her computer out of sleep mode.

"Party pooper." Cricket maneuvered her chair back to her own cubicle while still sitting in it.

Lindsey pushed their conversation to the back of her mind so she could concentrate on work. At least she tried to. She heard the ping from an incoming text. She pulled her backpack out from under her desk and dug out her phone.

It was from Sarah. *Hi, Lindsey! I just wanted to say thanks for a great day yesterday. I truly enjoyed your company.*

Lindsey's mood brightened considerably. *Me too. Let's get together again, soon.* She reread it before hitting send to make sure it didn't sound too...too what? Too needy? Too desperate? Too pushy? She always seemed to be second-guessing herself when it came to Sarah.

What are you doing for Easter? Sarah responded.

Lindsey hadn't even thought about Easter. It was only a week away. She'd spent most holidays with Cricket's family when she was young and then Tina's family when they'd been together. This would be her first Easter alone. *No plans,* she typed.

Would you like to join me at my parents'? My whole family will be there.

Lindsey didn't have to think about it long. *That would be great. Thanks.*

Wonderful. I'll call this evening so we can work out the details. Sarah replied.

Lindsey sent a smiley face and a bunny emoji back. She would think about Cricket's question later. She couldn't help but grin. She had something to look forward to.

❖

Sarah put her phone back in her desk drawer. She was glad Lindsey had accepted her invitation. It felt good to have a *buddy.* A friend. There were still some things that felt strange as she stepped back into her life. But most of it felt good. Being with Lindsey certainly felt good.

"What's the smile for?" She hadn't noticed that Cindy was standing in the doorway of her office.

"Nothing. What's up?"

Cindy took several steps into the room and placed a folder on Sarah's desk. "Here's the report you asked for."

"Thanks."

Cindy was silent but made no move to leave.

"Anything else?" Sarah asked. Cindy joined the company a year ago. They were co-workers. Acquaintances. But Sarah wouldn't have classified them as friends. They probably could have been if Sarah had been open to it. She hadn't been open to much the last couple of years.

Cindy squinted and tilted her head. "There's something different about you today. I'm trying to figure out what it is."

Sarah crossed her arms and leaned back in her chair. "And have you come to any conclusions?"

"It's the smile."

Sarah leaned forward. "What?"

"Your smile…" She hesitated.

"Go on," Sarah said, curious to see what Cindy had observed.

Cindy cleared her throat, but still hesitated.

Sarah raised her eyebrows, urging Cindy to respond.

"Okay. You haven't smiled much since I've known you." Cindy put her hands up. "Not that you didn't have every reason not to smile. Today you're smiling. And it's a real smile."

Sarah was surprised. She hadn't realized that her smile didn't register as genuine up until now. She was at a loss for words.

"I don't mean to offend you."

Sarah shook her head. "No. No. You didn't offend me. You're right. I haven't been very happy the last few years. But…"

Cindy seemed to be waiting patiently for Sarah to finish.

"But I guess things are starting to change."

"I'm glad," Cindy said. "Well, I should get back to work."

"Me too," Sarah said. "And, Cindy, thank you."

"Anytime." Cindy closed the door on her way out.

Sarah's thoughts went back to Lindsey. Easter was almost a week away. Was there something she could invite Lindsey to before that? Lindsey seemed to have become very important to her—very fast. Most—maybe all—of her friendships had evolved over time. Not so with Lindsey. They seemed to have jumped into this friendship with both feet right from the start.

Robin had said it was meant to be, and Sarah was starting to believe that.

She opened her desk drawer, retrieved her phone, and sent another text. *What time do you get out of work on Thursday?*

It took Lindsey nearly an hour to respond. *Sorry for the delay. Busy day. I work till five every day.*

Dinner at my house? I promise to feed you something better than pizza.

There's something better than pizza? Lindsey responded. *I doubt that.*

Sarah laughed. *Good point. I promise something almost as good as pizza.*

Now you have my attention.

Six o'clock. My place. Food. Wine. Good conversation.

You had me at wine. I'll be there. Can I bring anything?

Sarah thought about it for a few moments. She had no idea what she was going to cook. She hadn't cooked for anyone but herself for a long time and that was usually something quick and easy. That wouldn't do. *Nope.* She typed. *Just bring your beautiful face.* She wondered if Lindsey would take that the wrong way. She decided it was fine and hit send.

I always bring my face with me. I'm kind of attached to it... or is it attached to me? Lindsey replied.

Sarah laughed. Lindsey seemed to do that a lot...make Sarah laugh. *You're insane.*

I prefer crazy.

Ok crazy. Time for me to get back to work. See you on Thursday. I'm sure we'll talk before then. At least Sarah hoped they would. She sent a smiley face and a pizza emoji.

Lindsey sent back several food emojis.

Sarah opened the folder that Cindy dropped off but didn't bother reading it. Her attention went back to Lindsey and what she could make them for dinner. Several ideas came and went. Chicken. Everybody liked chicken. Didn't they? *Do you like chicken?* She texted Lindsey.

Doesn't everybody? Lindsey responded.

That was my exact thought. Sarah texted. *Any dietary restrictions?* Sarah had work to do. Why was she more interested in chatting with Lindsey?

Hmm. Nothing hot.

You like your food cold? Sarah responded.

Let me rephrase. Nothing spicy hot.

Oooooh! Now I understand. That makes more sense. Go back to work. Your boss is probably tired of you texting all day. Sarah knew she should take her own advice. She should be reading the report she'd been waiting for.

LOL! Good thinking.

Sarah turned her phone off before putting it back in her desk drawer. She knew if she didn't, she would be tempted to continue texting, which wouldn't be good for her job performance. Not that she couldn't turn the phone back on. But this way it at least meant she had to think about it. That didn't stop her from thinking about Lindsey, though.

CHAPTER EIGHT

Sarah stuck the temperature probe in the chicken breast. Good thing it had the correct cooking temperatures printed on it or she would have no idea what temperature chicken needed to reach so she wouldn't poison her guest. Julie was the main cook in the family, and Sarah never appreciated it until she was gone. "I sure could use your help with this." Sarah looked up at the ceiling as if Julie was hovering above her. "Of course, if you were here, I never would have met Lindsey and wouldn't be struggling with this dinner." The words brought a pang of—of what? Guilt? Grief? Anger? Maybe all of the above. She seemed to be having a lot of these *pang moments.*

She shook off the feelings and read the thermometer. One hundred thirty. Not cooked enough. She slipped the pan back into the oven and hoped the potatoes surrounding the chicken wouldn't burn.

She jumped when the doorbell rang. The laugh that bubbled up her throat was both out of embarrassment—even though no one saw her startled reaction—and excitement at seeing Lindsey. It felt good to have a friend again.

She searched the counter for a dishtowel to wipe her hands on and discovered it tucked into the waistband of her pants. "I'm losing my mind," she said as she walked to the door. "And I'm talking to myself. That can't be good."

She was surprised to find two young men—boys, really—dressed in black pants, white shirts, and narrow black ties. They each held a thick black book and she suspected they were there to preach some religion. She didn't have time for this crap. Not that she thought religion was crap. It just wasn't for her. She preferred more of a spiritual, personal approach to her relationship with the creator.

"Good afternoon, ma'am," the taller boy said. "Can you spare a few minutes—"

"I'm sorry. I can't. I'm expecting company." Sarah cut him off.

"We would be happy to share the good news with your company as well."

Sarah could see Lindsey coming up the walk behind the boys. "Yeah. No. Not today."

"Am I interrupting anything?" Lindsey asked as she reached the door.

One of the boys turned toward her. "Good afternoon, ma'am. We're here to share—"

"Sharing is great," Lindsey responded before he finished. She looked at Sarah.

Sarah raised her eyebrows and shook her head slightly, hoping her message that she was trying to get rid of the boys got through.

"But I'm gay and your church doesn't seem to like people like me," Lindsey told them.

Both boys' mouths dropped open. They seemed to be at a loss for words. One of them cleared his throat. "Umm," he finally said. "The Bible—"

"Preaches love," Lindsey said. "At least Jesus did. The Old Testament, not so much. And I would love it if I could get past you. I have dinner reservations at this fine entablement."

The boys parted—like the Red Sea, Sarah thought and giggled to herself. Lindsey crossed the threshold. She turned back to the boys. "I appreciate your efforts. I hope you have a great day." She gently closed the door behind her.

"Wow," Sarah said. "You handled that great. I never know what to say to get rid of them."

"I hope you don't mind that I said I was gay."

"Not at all. Julie always had a rainbow flag in front of the house. I took it in for the winter and never got around to putting it back up."

"I would imagine that would detour the religious types from knocking on your door."

"You would think, huh? But they actually tried to *save* us from the perverseness that is sure to send us to hell." Sarah used air quotes. "Their intentions are good. Their execution, not so much. Some of them are relentless."

"Do I smell something burning?" Lindsey asked.

"Oh shit." Sarah rushed back to the kitchen, followed closely by Lindsey. She grabbed two potholders and pulled the pan of chicken and potatoes from the oven. She set it on the trivet on the counter and peered in. Nothing in the pan seemed to be burnt.

Lindsey stepped closer, reached around Sarah, and removed a pot from the back burner. Smoke billowed out when she lifted the lid, sending the smoke alarm into a frenzy. She quickly put the cover back on, but the room had already filled with smoke.

Sarah stared in horror at the pot as if she could will it not to be burnt. Even more horrific was the fact that she burst into tears.

Lindsey took only a moment to step closer and wrap her arms around Sarah. "Hey," she said, loud enough to be heard over the screaming smoke detector. "It's not that bad. I love the taste of burnt brussels sprouts. Although the smell isn't great."

That made Sarah cry even harder. *What the hell is wrong with me? It's not like it's spilt milk. Oh wait, we aren't supposed to cry over that either.* The thought made her giggle through her tears and created the perfect combination for a round of hiccups.

"Sugar," Lindsey said.

"What?" Sarah asked through the sobs and hiccups.

Lindsey pulled back enough to look into Sarah's eyes. "My grandmother would put a little sugar on my tongue whenever I had the hiccups. Worked like a charm. Hold on." Lindsey released Sarah and grabbed a wooden spoon from the utensil holder on the counter. She reached up with it and hit the button on the smoke detector silencing it. Then she pulled a paper towel from the roll, wiped Sarah's cheeks, and dabbed at the corner of her eyes.

Sarah wasn't sure if she should be grateful or die from embarrassment. She had no idea what had come over her. One thing she did know was how comforting Lindsey's arms around her had felt. More than comforting. Like coming home. Like she belonged in those arms. Fresh tears fell as guilt replaced the other feelings. She hiccupped again. This was getting ridiculous. Crying, hiccupping, giggling at the stupidity of it all.

"Where's your sugar?" Lindsey asked.

Sarah pulled a plastic container from one of the cabinets.

Lindsey opened two drawers before finding a spoon. She scooped a half a spoonful of sugar and aimed it at Sarah's mouth. "Open."

Sarah did as she was told, and Lindsey spooned the sugar in. The hiccups stopped almost immediately. Lindsey brushed away the last few tears on Sarah's face with the side of her thumb.

"What's going on?" Lindsey asked, tilting her head and looking directly into Sarah's eyes.

"Damned if I know. I wanted everything to be perfect. And I blew it."

Lindsey pulled her back into a hug. Sarah could get used to this if the guilt would just release its hold on her. How could she feel anything for another woman after Julie? It just wasn't right.

"You didn't blow it. We open some windows. Throw the burnt food outside in the trash can and eat"—she turned to see what was in the pan on the counter—"chicken and potatoes. I was lying about liking burnt brussels sprouts anyway."

Sarah laughed. "You aren't willing to even try them after all the trouble I went through?"

"I like you a lot and would do just about anything for you. But eating the black things in that pot is where I have to draw the line."

"It does smell awful, doesn't it?" She reluctantly pulled herself out of the warmth of Lindsey's arms. She opened the only window in the kitchen, turned the exhaust fan over the stove on, and took the pot out the back door to the garbage can. She removed the cover, peered in at the burnt mess and tossed the whole thing into the trash.

"Where's the pan?" Lindsey asked when she returned.

"It was hopeless. I threw it out."

"Why? A little baking soda and soak and it would have come out good as new."

"Is there anything you don't know?" Sarah asked. "You can cure hiccups, clean burnt pans, and comfort a crazy woman who cries for no reason. Not to mention making horrible noises stop with the touch of a wooden spoon."

Lindsey laughed.

It went straight to Sarah's heart and the ping of guilt followed right behind. She took a step back and looked away.

"What's wrong?" Lindsey asked.

There was no way Sarah could tell her the truth, but she didn't want to lie either. It took her several moments to answer. "I'm embarrassed. I messed everything up and then cried like a baby." It was close enough to the truth.

"Hey," Lindsey said. "Look at me."

Sarah brought her eyes to Lindsey's, and she saw the kindness there.

"You have nothing to be embarrassed about. Burned food isn't the end of the world and everyone cries now and then." She raised her eyebrows. "Even someone as amazing as me."

Sarah couldn't help but smile. "You *are* pretty amazing." She truly believed that.

"You forgot modest."

"You're modest alright. Probably the most amazingly modest person I know." And someone I'd like to get to know a lot better. She was surprised that the thought didn't bring another round of guilt.

"Now," Lindsey said, taking Sarah's hand. "What have we learned here today?"

The gesture and the question surprised Sarah. She thought about it for a moment, trying to ignore the tingling sensation that went from her hand to her center. "Well," she started. "We learned that you're amazing and modest—as we've just discussed. We've learned that a burnt pan can be cleaned and that there is no use crying over ruined brussels sprouts and that they smell horrible when you let all the water boil away."

"Anything else?"

"Everyone cries sometimes."

"Very good."

"Were you a teacher in another life?"

Linsey dropped Sarah's hand and brought her own hand to her chin. Sarah missed the warmth of it immediately.

"Hmm. I know I was Cleopatra, Joan of Arc, and Mary Magdalene in my past lives. By the way, when I was Mary, I was not a hooker, like some would want you to believe. I was a businesswoman. Which in those days was almost as bad. But…" She paused. "I don't think I was a teacher."

"You believe in past lives?"

"Yes. Do you?"

"I believe we should put this food on plates and eat before it's ice cold. She got a sharp knife from the wooden block on the counter—a gift she'd given to Julie on their fifth anniversary—a very expensive gift. She'd thought it was clever, as the fifth anniversary was wood. She sliced into one of the pieces of chicken to make sure it was cooked through. She figured the thermometer wouldn't be very accurate seeing the chicken had been out of the oven too long. It looked cooked enough not to give them salmonella or was it E. coli? She always got those things mixed up. Pork could give you trichinosis. That one she knew for sure. Her mother always cooked pork chops to shoe leather consistency to avoid it. That's why she hated pork to this day.

"Where'd you go just now?" Lindsey asked.

"What?"

"You were somewhere in your head."

"Oh. I was just thinking about all the ways undercooked meat can kill you."

"You aren't planning on killing me with raw meat, are you?"

This was why she liked Lindsey so much. She was funny and said the most unexpected things. "Oh no. I would never do that. It's too unpredictable. It might not kill you or it could just give you a major case of the runs. I would do something quick and clean."

"Clean?"

Sarah plated up the chicken and potatoes. "Yes. You know. A gunshot would be very messy. Blood, guts, brains."

"Yeah. I could see that. What can I do to help?"

"With the murder plan?" Sarah smirked.

"No. With dinner?"

"There is silverware in the last drawer." She nodded her chin in that direction. "Where you found the spoon."

Lindsey retrieved two forks and two knives. "I never took you for a serial killer."

"Oh. I'm not. But if I was, I could probably get away with it." She brought the food to the adjoining dining room and set it on the table. She continued gathering what they needed until the table was set and they were sitting across from each other.

"I'm glad you're not a killer, by the way. And how would you get away with it if you were?"

"Deep grave. That's the secret." She cut her chicken into bite-sized pieces.

"How so?"

"Ever notice how the killer is always caught when they find the body in a shallow grave. Come on, people. Put a little effort into it. If they buried the body in a deep grave, no one would ever find it." She poured wine into each of their glasses, held hers up, and waited for Lindsey to do the same. "Here's to deep graves."

"And to letting my friends know that if I ever go missing, they need to dig down deep to find me." They clinked their glasses together.

"Good thinking."

Lindsey took a sip of her wine, letting it swirl around her taste buds. It was good. Very good. "This is excellent."

"Thanks. Julie picked it out."

Lindsey was confused. She wasn't sure if she should ask about it or not.

"I mean, before she died, Julie had a nice stash of wine. I haven't really opened any of it until now. I've had wine since then, of course. But I've mostly just bought the cheap stuff for myself. I went through quite a few bottles the first few months—" She stopped suddenly. "That's probably not a good thing to admit."

Lindsey had done the opposite after Tina left—avoided alcohol, afraid she could end up with a drinking problem. Instead, she buried herself in food, movies, and the occasional joint. "Hey, we do what we need to do to get by. No judgment."

"Thanks. Do you really believe in past lives?" Sarah asked, obviously changing the subject. "You don't really think you were all those famous people, do you?"

"Yes and no. Yes, I believe in past lives. No, I don't really think I was a famous person." She paused. "Have you ever met someone and from the first moment you felt like you've known them forever?"

"Yes. It's…" Sarah paused so long that Lindsey was sure she wouldn't finish her sentence. "…you," she said at last.

Lindsey hadn't thought about it, but she felt the same way.

"So, what does that mean?"

"First, let me say, me too. I believe it means we've known each other in a past life." She searched Sarah's face for some kind of reaction. She didn't share her beliefs with too many people. She'd learned from experience that some took it the wrong way and labeled her a kook. She didn't want Sarah thinking that about her. She couldn't quite read Sarah's expression. "Tell me what you're thinking," she said.

"I'm just trying to think of anyone else I've felt an instant connection to."

Lindsey wondered if she should ask about Julie, if she'd felt that way when they first met. She decided against it. She didn't want to see Sarah cry again. That was hard to witness, and she didn't know if talking about Julie would do that. "And?" Lindsey asked, deciding it was a much less intimidating way to ask.

"My mom," Sarah said, with a giggle. "I liked her from the start. What about you? Did you feel that when you met Tina?"

Lindsey laughed. "Hell no. I didn't even like her when we first met."

"Maybe that should have been your first clue."

"You're absolutely right." Lindsey sliced into her chicken and took a bite. It was starting to get cold, but she didn't mind. The conversation felt simulating. Warming. Almost intimate.

"Then how did you end up together?"

Lindsey told the story of them meeting at a party and Tina practically throwing herself at Lindsey. Lindsey didn't give her another thought until they met again a few months later in a gardening class and hit it off. Tina had even apologized for her behavior at the party, chalking it up to too much alcohol.

"Why were you taking a gardening class?" Sarah asked. "I didn't know you liked to garden." She took a bite of her food.

"I used to help my grandmother with her garden. Thought I might try it myself sometime. I love planting things and watching them grow."

"And did you? Have you? Gardened since then?"

"I've got a ton of houseplants. I didn't really have a place to plant a garden until this year. I did learn how to propagate fig cuttings in the class. I learned how to propagate roses, actually. I figured out the rest from YouTube videos. I lived in an apartment most of my adult life, so a garden was out of the question. I bought myself a house several months ago. So, this will be the year for it."

"Julie did our gardening. Flowers mostly. Roses. The painting that I showed you, with the flowers—those were from her garden."

"Beautiful. And the flowers lining your walkway out front?"

"Yep. Planted those too. I am afraid they have been poorly neglected since she's been gone. But they're faithful. They come up every spring anyway."

"Perennials." Lindsey finished the last bite of food on her plate. She hadn't even realized she'd eaten it all, she was so wrapped up in their conversation.

"What?"

"The flowers in front. They come up every year because they're perennials. Julie must have put down some sort of weed block, unless you've been out there weeding."

Sarah shook her head. "Nope. Not me. I wouldn't mind planting some flowers in the backyard. The gardens have been empty for a while now. So, there must not have been perennials planted there."

"You'll have to wait till after the last frost. We're zone six B."

"And that means?"

Lindsey finished off her wine and Sarah refilled her glass. "Thanks. If memory serves—and sometimes it doesn't—the last frost date is around the middle of May. You don't want to plant annuals till after that or they could freeze."

"How come the perennials don't freeze?"

Lindsey took her time explaining the difference and answering Sarah's questions.

"I got some seed catalogs in the mail. Remind me before the next time I see you and I'll bring them. It's a little late to start seeds, but it will give you an idea of what kind of flowers you might like. We can pick some up from a nursery."

"You don't need them?"

"No. I might start seeds next year. This year I'm buying the plants. I guess the time got away from me." She sipped her wine. "Speaking of time, how are the paintings coming?"

"Good. I have three finished. And another one started."

Lindsey was impressed. "That's great. Do I get to see them?"

Sarah seemed to think about it for a few moments. "How about you come to the art opening and see them there, framed, in all their glory?"

Lindsey was disappointed and at the same time thrilled to get a personal invitation to the opening. "Sure. That would be great. Are you happy with them?"

"Believe it or not, I am."

"Why wouldn't I believe it?" Sarah was such a talented artist. There was no way she wouldn't be happy with her work.

"I wasn't sure I could paint again. I mean it had been quite a while. I was sure nothing would happen when I picked up a brush. I struggled so much when I started the first one. I thought I might have to cancel the show. I have some older paintings to put in it, but it wouldn't have been enough."

Lindsey found that hard to believe. You didn't see talent like Sarah's every day, and it would have been a shame if it had gone away. "From what I've seen, you have more than conquered it. You've mastered it. I can't believe you don't do this for a living."

"It's hard to make a living from just your art. I like to do the little things in life that take money—like buy groceries and keeping the electricity on. Julie said she would take a second job to pay the bills so I could do art full-time. But I said no. It was more important to spend time with her than pursue an art career while she was out working all the time." Sarah looked sad and Lindsey wanted to put her arms around her. But she'd done that twice in the kitchen and if she continued doing it, Sarah might get the wrong idea—or the right idea and not like it. "Anyway," Sarah continued. "Now I'm glad I made that decision."

Lindsey wasn't sure how to respond, so she just nodded.

"I'm sorry," Sarah said.

"For what?"

"For bringing the mood down and talking about Julie."

"Nonsense. You're allowed to talk about Julie. Listen, she was a huge part of your life. I don't want you to have to censor yourself when we're talking. You can tell me about her or anything. I mean that. Anything."

It was Sarah that initiated the physical contact this time when she laid her hand over Lindsey's and rubbed it. Lindsey was tempted to close her eyes against the feelings it awakened in her, but she didn't.

"Thank you," Sarah said. "I appreciate that more than you know. So many people—friends—most of them ex-friends now—wouldn't let me talk about Julie at all. It was as if they wanted to forget she existed."

"I don't think that was their intention. I've found that people avoid conversations when they don't know what to say."

"You're probably right, but one by one, they seemed to have dropped out of my life. But I'm so happy I've met you."

"Right back atcha." *More than you'll ever know. And I'm never going to tell you that.*

CHAPTER NINE

Easter dinner at Sarah's parents' called for something nicer than her usual blouse and jeans. She owned exactly two dresses, and neither one fit right. The eight pounds she'd gained after Tina left her—okay it was actually ten—made the dresses too tight in the bust and waist. A bigger bust is a good thing, she told herself. But a tight dress wasn't.

She finally settled on a pair of gray dress pants and a purple—lavender really—blouse with a lacey neckline. She added matching earrings and a necklace. Her good shoes were in the back of the closet—way back—and she messed up her hair trying to reach them.

A quick brush through, a spritz of hairspray, and a light layer of mascara and she was out the door. She grabbed the plant she'd bought for Sarah's mother, hyacinths, from the front porch and got in her car, setting the plant on the floor on the passenger side.

She turned the key and...nothing. The car didn't start. She made sure it was in park and tried again. "Well, crap. Now what?" Banging her hands against the steering wheel and turning the key again didn't work. She pressed Sarah's contact number on her phone.

"Hello."

"Sarah, I seem to have a problem. My car won't start. I'm afraid I'm not going to make it."

"Do you have Triple A?"

"I don't."

"I do. How about I come and get you, we can call Triple A, and have them meet us there. I can pretend it's my car and we'll see if they can get it going."

"No. That's too much. You would be late for your parents' dinner."

"It's no big deal. They don't eat right away anyways. And even if they did it wouldn't be as much fun without you there. Text me the address and I'll see you in about twenty minutes."

"Okay. If you're sure."

"I'm sure."

Lindsey turned the key one more time just in case there was a miracle in store for her. There wasn't. She sent Sarah her address and trudged back into the house to wait. Sarah arrived eighteen minutes later.

"You look amazing," she said as she gave her a hug. Lindsey's hugs were the best and Sarah looked forward to them. She put her whole self into it, not just one of those lean your shoulders forward and pat someone on the back kind of hugs she'd gotten used to from some of her other friends.

"Thank you. You do too."

Sarah had taken her time picking out her outfit for the day. Besides it being Easter, she wanted to look nice for Lindsey, which made no sense when she thought about it, but did it anyway. "Triple A should be here in about ten minutes," Sarah said.

Lindsey gave her a quick tour of the house while they waited. It was much smaller than Sarah's, but nicely decorated. Cute. It seemed to fit Lindsey's personality.

"This," Lindsey said. "Is my plant room." She opened the door and gestured for Sarah to go in.

"Your plants get their own room? Cool."

"And here are the figs I was telling you about." Lindsey lifted a clear plastic cup from a shallow bin. It had a stick stuck in the dirt—if that was dirt—with a tiny bit of green growth at the top. "Look," Lindsey said. "Little tiny roots." She sounded like a proud parent.

Sarah could see white stringy-looking things poking through the dirt. Roots.

"And it's starting to get leaves. That's a good sign. But you don't want too many before the roots."

"How big does it have to be before you can replant it?"

"I need to wait till it has more roots. This one is doing the best. I have five altogether."

"Are you going to plant them all in the yard?" Sarah asked.

"No. I'll just keep the best one or two and probably give the others away. It needs probably a year in a pot before it's big enough to plant in the ground."

Sarah paused to read an incoming text. "Mechanic will be here in a couple of minutes," she said.

"We can wait on the porch swing if you want," Lindsey responded. "By the way, I am really grateful for the help."

"Anytime, and it's such a beautiful day, the swing would be perfect." Sarah followed Lindsey outside. The swing was small, just big enough for the two of them with no room to spare. Sarah's leg rested against Lindsey, and it felt so—she tried to figure out the feeling—so natural. That was it. As if they'd known each other for years. Or maybe it was that past life thing Lindsey had talked about. Whatever it was, she felt so comfortable in Lindsey's presence.

They didn't have to wait long for Triple A to arrive. Sarah showed the guy—Jimmy, his name tag said—her card and told him which car wouldn't start. He hooked some gizmo up to the battery. "There's your problem right there. Battery's dead."

"Can you jump start it?" Lindsey asked.

He scratched at the stubble on his chin. "I could but it's not gonna last. See here." He pointed at the gauge. "That number should be much higher. You're gonna need a new battery."

"Can you replace it?" Sarah asked.

"I could, but I don't have the right one with me. I'm gonna have to go back to the shop and get one. I got one more call I need to go on first. I'm thinkin' it'll be about an hour."

"We have a dinner we need to get to," Sarah said. "Any chance we can pay you for the battery and have you put it in while we're gone?" She looked at Lindsey to make sure that was okay with her. She didn't seem to object.

More chin scratching. "I suppose I could do that. You're gonna have to leave me the key so I can check it."

"We can do that," Lindsey said. "You can leave the key in the mail slot in my door. Can you take a check?"

"I can just leave you a bill," Jimmy said. "You got like thirty days to pay."

"Great," Sarah said. "Lindsey, you okay with that?"

"Yep."

"Good. Thank you, Jimmy."

"Sure thing."

They waited until he left before climbing into Sarah's car. "Are you sure you want to do this?" Lindsey asked. "I can try to get an Uber home, so you don't have to drive me."

"Don't be ridiculous," Sarah said. "I don't mind at all." Besides, she thought, it means I get to spend more time with you.

"Thank you."

"You don't have to thank me. I'm happy to help and happy that you are joining us for Easter dinner."

"Me too. Oh wait," Lindsey said.

Sarah watched as Lindsey got out of the car, opened the front passenger side door of her own car, and retrieved a plant.

"You shouldn't have," Sarah said as Lindsey slid back onto the seat.

"It's for your mom."

"I knew that," Sarah said with a smile. She wished she'd thought to bring something too. Oh well, guess it would just be Lindsey making a good impression. She was okay with that. They chitchatted about nothing and everything on the ride to Sarah's parents' house. The conversation flowed so effortlessly.

The front door of her parents' house was unlocked, and they let themselves in. There was no one inside.

"Must be in the backyard," Sarah said.

Lindsey set the plant she was carrying on the counter as they passed through the kitchen.

"Hey, you two. You're just in time for the Easter egg hunt," Sarah's father said once they'd stepped out the back door. He gave them both a quick hug.

Everyone was watching as Greg and Wally scoured the lawn, each with a basket swinging from the crook of their arm. "I found one," Wally called out.

The excitement in his voice made Sarah smile and she looked over at Lindsey as if to share the joy she felt. Lindsey smiled back and it warmed Sarah's heart.

Sarah glanced over at her mother across the yard. Her mother had obviously watched the exchange, smiled, and nodded in the direction of Lindsey. Sarah knew her mother well enough to know that there was some meaning in that nod. Meaning that Sarah had tried to squash the last time they were all together. She would have to have another talk with her and explain in no uncertain terms that she and Lindsey were just friends.

She turned the word over in her mind. Maybe *best friends* was closer to the truth. Could you be best friends with someone that you'd only met a short time ago? Apparently yes. Because Lindsey felt like more than just a *friend*.

She didn't want to think about it beyond that. In another time there might have been more. But she'd lost the love of her life. There was no replacing that. She wasn't willing to try. Not with Lindsey. Not with anyone. Besides, Lindsey had made no moves or voiced any interest in being more than friends. So, it was a moot point, anyway.

"Way to go, Greg," Lindsey called out when he found three brightly colored eggs in a row.

Sarah's dad helped Wally find the last two. He came running over to Sarah and Lindsey, proudly holding up his basket. "Look how many I found, Aunt Sarah."

She peered into the basket. "Wow. Great job, buddy."

"Look," he said to Lindsey.

"That's wonderful. So many."

"Yep." He trotted off to show his mother.

Sarah's mother crossed the yard and approached them. "Well, hello, you two." She gave them both a hug. "Lindsey, so nice you could join us again."

"I really appreciate you including me, Mrs. Os—Judy."

"Of course. Come on in." She held the door open as everyone filed into the house. She spotted the plant on the counter. "Sarah, did you bring this?"

Sarah shook her head. "Nope. That was all Lindsey. I'm not that thoughtful."

"Thank you, Lindsey. That was very kind," Sarah's mother said.

"You're welcome."

Lindsey caught Sarah's eye and smiled. Sarah smiled back, so happy that Lindsey was there to share the day.

"What can I help with?" Lindsey asked.

"Not a thing," Sarah's mother answered. "Everybody out of the kitchen while I finish up dinner. Sarah, can you help me?"

Sarah was momentarily confused. "Sure. What do you need me to do?" she asked once everyone had left the kitchen.

"Nothing. I want to ask you about Lindsey."

Sarah leaned against the counter, folded her arms, and sucked in her bottom lip waiting for the question she was sure she didn't want to hear.

"Have you noticed the way she looks at you?" She slipped a pair of oven mitts on her hands.

"What are you talking about?"

"Honey, I think she has feelings for you." She opened the oven, removed a pan with a spiral ham in it, and set the pan on top of the stove.

Sarah wasn't sure if the heat she felt rising in her was from the pan or from the irritation she felt at her mother's statement. "That's crazy. I've told you before that we're just friends."

"Are you sure that's how she feels?"

"We haven't talked about it, but why would she think anything different?"

"I don't know." She stirred something in a pan on the back burner and spooned what Sarah surmised was brown sugar glaze over the ham. Then she turned her full attention to Sarah. "I just don't want to see anyone get hurt. I'm wondering if you should have a talk with her." She paused. "That is if you're sure you aren't feeling something for her too."

How could she feel anything for anyone other than Julie? Julie hadn't been gone that long. Okay, two years *was* a long time. An eternity when you're missing someone. But still. "I'm not. I've told you that already."

"I know you have. But there seems to be a connection there that I'm not sure you're allowing."

Sarah shook her head. "Allowing? You either have feelings or you don't. There's no allowing."

"I'm not trying to get you upset, Sarah. I'm only asking you to pay attention—to your feelings and to Lindsey's."

Sarah opened her mouth to object but closed it again. Was there anything to what her mother was saying? It might be worth exploring. She thought back to some of the physical sensations she'd experienced when Lindsey touched or hugged her. She'd chalked them up to loneliness. Nothing more. Could she have been wrong? The thought of it made her stomach sour.

"Sarah," her mother said. "Just think about it. That's all I'm saying."

"Okay." After that conversation how could she do anything *but* think about it.

"Would you mind setting the dining room table for me? You can ask Lindsey to help if you want."

Sarah nodded. She knew that Easter dinner called for the good dishes stored in the china cabinet in the dining room. She set about the task tossing around the thoughts her mother had planted in her head. She hadn't come to any conclusions by the time she finished. She also hadn't noticed that Lindsey had come up behind her.

"Need any help?" Lindsey said, so close to her ear that it sent shivers down her spine.

There. That feeling. What was that? That was what she needed to figure out.

"Sarah?"

Sarah turned. She was so close to Lindsey that she could feel Lindsey's breath on her cheek. Her eyes, against her will went to Lindsey's lips. Had she noticed how full they were before? How soft they looked? Did she want to kiss them?

"Sarah?" Lindsey repeated. "You okay?"

Sarah blinked a few times and brought her eyes back up to Lindsey's. "Um, yes. Sorry. Just lost in thought."

"Oookaaay," Lindsey drew the word out. "Anything interesting?"

"Huh?"

"Were your thoughts interesting? Never mind. Need any help?"

Sarah took a step back and hit her hip on the edge of the table. *Damn. That hurt. Get ahold of yourself.* "Nope. Just finished."

"Story of my life. Always a step behind," Lindsey said with a smile.

"Maybe I'm the one that's a step behind." *Did I just say that out loud? Damn it. Please don't ask what I mean by that.*

"What do you mean?"

Shit. I said not to ask. Think quick. "Nothing." *Great answer.*

"You sure you're okay? You seem flustered."

"I'm fine." *Why did Mom have to plant those thoughts in my brain? Okay, Sarah, get out of your head and into the conversation.*

Lindsey wasn't so sure about that. She didn't know what went on in the kitchen between Sarah and her mother, but whatever it was seemed to have affected Sarah. She didn't think she should push it. "Your father was just telling me how proud he is of your art," Lindsey said, trying to change the subject.

"Yes. He's always been one of my biggest cheerleaders." Sarah smiled and Lindsey was glad to see a glimmer of the old Sarah come through.

"Your family is great," Lindsey said. She was a little jealous if she was being honest with herself. It was the kind of family she'd always wished she had when she was growing up.

"I know," Sarah said. "They're the best."

Judy came in carrying a platter of ham that she set in the middle of the table. "I can use some help bringing in the rest of the food."

"Sure, Mom. You sit. Lindsey and I will get it," Sarah said.

It only took a few minutes for them to get everything on the table and have everyone seated.

"Lindsey, come sit here next to me and Sarah sit on the other side of her," Judy said.

Lindsey nodded and followed Sarah to her seat. She took Judy's and Sarah's hands as Wally said grace. Lindsey winked at him when he finished, and he giggled. Yes, Sarah was lucky indeed to have this wonderful family and she was so lucky that they were kind enough to include her.

Sarah held onto her hand several long seconds after Lindsey had let go of Judy's hand and Sarah had dropped Mary's hand on the other side of her. It felt nice but confusing. Even more so when Sarah suddenly dropped her hand as if it was on fire. Lindsey looked over at her but couldn't catch her eye.

"Here you go, Lindsey," Judy said, handing her a bowl of mashed potatoes. "Don't be shy. Eat up." The hustle and bustle of eating with a large family kicked in as the food went around the table. The conversations were steady, the food was good, and the gratitude Lindsey felt was enormous.

"I really appreciate you including me in your family celebration," Lindsey said on the ride back to her house.

Sarah smiled at her. "I'm glad you were there."

The rest of the ride was quiet. It wasn't uncomfortable but it was unusual. There was rarely a lull in the conversation when they were together. Lindsey wondered what Sarah was thinking. Her whole demeaner seemed to have change after she and her mother were alone in the kitchen. She wondered what that was all about.

CHAPTER TEN

Sarah had trouble falling asleep. She concluded after much thinking and rethinking that she did indeed have feelings for Lindsey beyond friendship. Feelings she didn't want to have. When she made the conscious decision to restart her life—a life without Julie—she hadn't intended to find a new relationship. Granted if she did want a relationship, Lindsey would fit the bill perfectly. She was kind, thoughtful, and funny. She made Sarah laugh and that seemed to have opened Sarah's heart. A heart that had been shattered to pieces on the day Julie died. Letting someone else put the pieces back together was a betrayal of Julie. Wasn't it?

A lot of people went on to have other relationships after losing a spouse. But Sarah wasn't other people. And it wasn't just anyone she'd lost. It was Julie. There was no replacing her. Sarah didn't even want to try. So that left the question—what to do with the feelings?

Nothing. There was nothing she would do with them. She'd shoved down her grief for quite a long while. She could shove these feelings down too. But what about what her mother had said? Lindsey looked like she had feelings for her, too. Was her mother right? If so, would it be fair to Lindsey to continue their friendship? That was more than her brain wanted to think about. Or was it her heart?

No. She wouldn't be cutting off her friendship with Lindsey. She would carry on as if nothing had changed—because it really hadn't. She would have to pay attention to the way she looked at Lindsey and even the way Lindsey looked at her. These feelings, hers and possibly Lindsey's, if her mother was right, would pass if they didn't act on them. And she had no intention of letting that happen.

Holding Lindsey's hand too long after Wally said grace, was a stupid mistake. She hoped Lindsey hadn't noticed, but she could feel Lindsey's eyes on her, and she avoided looking at her, hoping the moment would pass. It did and they carried on as if nothing had happened. She was lost in her head as she drove Lindsey home. Lindsey seemed to be unusually quiet as well. She might have been overwhelmed by all the commotion of Sarah's family. It could be a lot for someone who grew up without siblings.

She thought back to the first time Julie had dinner with her whole family. It was before Greg and Wally were born, and Mary wasn't married, so there was far less uproar. Sarah had been excited for her family to meet the person she was so in love with. Julie had been nervous, but the day went very well. And everyone loved her.

Sarah finally fell asleep sometime after two in the morning. Dreams of Julie mixed with dreams of Lindsey. Kissing. Who was kissing who in the dreams? Julie was kissing Lindsey as Sarah stood by and watched, jealousy seeping in around the edges. She pulled them apart and watched as Julie faded into the distant ether. Wisps of her danced back and then disappeared altogether. She was left alone with Lindsey. Lindsey reached a hand out to Sarah. Sarah stared at it, unsure of what to do. "Take it," Lindsey said. "Take it and let go of what was."

What was? Julie. Let go of Julie? Sarah turned in the direction Julie had disappeared. When she looked back to Lindsey, she was gone too. Sarah turned in circles searching. Searching for someone. Anyone. But there was no one there.

Everyone was gone and she was alone. But it wasn't Julie she wanted to reappear. It was Lindsey. She called out her name, but her voice was hoarse, and she could only manage a whisper. She tried again. Same results. The third time she was able to scream Lindsey's name and it woke her up.

Her heart pounded in her chest and her throat hurt. She sat up and turned on the lamp atop her nightstand. She blinked against the brightness of it. "What the hell was that?"

She closed her eyes and took a deep breath. "Julie, what does all this mean?" She shook her head. Are you trying to tell me something?" Tears streamed down her face. "Why the hell did you have to leave me?" It was so unfair.

She slipped out of bed, splashed cold water on her face in the bathroom, and went downstairs. She wandered aimlessly through the living room, into the kitchen and back again. Her heart ached and she didn't know what to do about it. It ached for Julie, but it also ached for Lindsey. And she wasn't sure why.

❖

"I'm telling you she was acting weird," Lindsey said to Cricket, Monday morning at work.

"In what way?" Cricket set her travel mug of coffee on her desk and looked up at Lindsey.

Lindsey leaned back against the cubicle wall. "She was really quiet, for one thing."

"You haven't known her that long. How do you know that's not normal for her?"

"It hasn't been so far. Something happened between her and her mother when they were alone in the kitchen."

"Did you ask her about it?"

"No. That didn't seem right."

"What else happened? Because her being quiet could mean a million different things."

Lindsey told Cricket about Sarah holding her hand and how suddenly she had dropped it, almost pushing Lindsey's hand away.

"Yeah. That's kind of weird. Maybe she was lost in her thoughts and just forgot to let go."

"She wasn't holding her sister's hand anymore. Just mine. And why would she drop it so fast?"

Cricket rocked back in her chair. "Why are you freaked out about this?"

Lindsey tilted her head. "I'm not freaked out."

"You're trying to analyze the hell out of it. If she's just a friend, why is it so important that she was quiet and dropped your hand?"

Lindsey considered her response carefully before answering. She knew she had strong feelings for Sarah, but saying it out loud—when she hadn't known Sarah that long—seemed childish. "Maybe I was just worried about her."

"Maybe you were just worried about yourself."

"What do you mean?" Lindsey asked, knowing exactly what she meant.

"You're afraid she is pulling back from you. Are you afraid her mother said something negative about you?"

Lindsey hadn't considered that. If Sarah's mother had anything against her, she certainly didn't show it. She was as warm as she'd been the first time she met her. "I don't think that's the case. But I don't know what else it could be." Lindsey had rolled all the possibilities around in her head all evening and then started again in the morning as soon as she opened her eyes. She was driving herself crazy and she knew it.

Cricket obviously knew it too. "If it continues, you should ask her about it."

"I don't know."

"Why? Afraid of pushing her away, or worse yet, learning that she's pushing you away?"

Lindsey wasn't ready to admit that to Cricket—or to herself. She didn't respond.

"That's okay," Cricket said. "I know the answer. You might want to analyze your own feelings instead of trying to figure out hers."

"How is it going with Trevor?" Lindsey needed Cricket to get out of her brain.

Cricket shook her head. "Nice deflection." She smiled. "It is wonderful, Lindsey. He's everything I thought he would be."

Lindsey put a hand on Cricket's shoulder. "Oh, I'm so happy for you."

They spent the next ten minutes talking about Trevor and how great he was. Lindsey was glad for the reprieve of her own thoughts, if only for a little while.

Back at her own desk, Lindsey sent a text to Sarah. *Thanks again for including me yesterday. I had a very nice time.* She found herself staring at her phone waiting for a response.

"Getting a lot done?" Jason came up behind her, making her jump.

"Umm. Yeah. Sorry." She put her phone in her backpack and turned her chair toward her computer. *Shit. I need to stop this obsessing.* But wishing it away didn't seem to work. She searched her mind to see if she had done or said anything that would have put Sarah off. No. The shift came after Sarah came out of the kitchen with her mother.

She did her best to keep her mind on her work for the next few hours and avoided checking her phone, but kept it close by in case a text came in. None did. *She's working, probably busy. Give her until this evening before you panic. Panic? What are you doing? There is no reason to panic.* "Shut up," she told her brain, under her breath.

"Are you talking to me?" Cricket said.

Lindsey jumped. People needed to stop sneaking up on her. "No. I'm talking to me."

"Why do you need to shut up? And why are you so jumpy?"

"Drinks after work?"

"That bad, huh?" Cricket asked.

"I just need to figure some stuff out and could use the company while I do it."

"Sure. Trevor and I were going to run off to Las Vegas to get married, but I guess that can wait."

Lindsey smiled. "Thanks. You're the best."

"I know. Just don't let it get around."

"I better scratch it off the bathroom stall, where I wrote it this morning."

"You can leave it, as long as you didn't put my phone number too." Cricket said.

"Now you tell me. Do you have a black Sharpie I can borrow?"

"I'll have to look. I usually do my bathroom graffiti with nail polish. Did you walk to work today?"

"Yep."

"Do you need to go home for anything before we go out?"

"Nope."

"Okay. Let me know when you're ready."

Lindsey nodded. "Thanks."

The rest of the workday seemed to last forever. There was still no text from Sarah by the time they got to Mulligan's. It was only a couple of blocks from work, and they never watered down the drinks like some of the other bars they had checked out. It had changed hands a couple of years ago and the new owner had made a lot of upgrades to the place. The new barstools were nicely padded and much more comfortable than the old ones.

"Talk," Cricket said while they waited for their drinks.

"I don't know," Lindsey said. She was glad the new owner had taken out the large mirror behind the bar. She hated looking up and catching her own reflection. She always found it distracting.

"I canceled my elopement for you, and you don't know what you want to talk about? What's going on?"

"Why am I so fixated on Sarah? I mean, it seemed to be going great until yesterday and today I sent her a text and she never responded. I don't know what to think."

"Well, you're obviously thinking something."

"I'm thinking that her mother said something to her that's making her pull away from me."

"You said you think her mother likes you. So, what else could she have said?"

Lindsey took a long swig of her gin and tonic as soon as the bartender set it in front of her. "Thanks." She turned back to Cricket. "Why else would Sarah pull away?"

"Let's back up here," Cricket said. "Instead of trying to figure out how Sarah or her mother feels about you, how do you feel about Sarah?"

"I like her," Lindsey said.

"Just like?"

"If you're asking if I'm in love with her, the answer is no."

Cricket swirled the liquid in her glass but didn't take a drink. "What about somewhere in between? Do you like her more than like?"

She didn't even have to think about it. "Yes." Was her simple answer.

"Does she know that?" Cricket sipped her drink. Lindsey didn't know how she could drink martinis. The taste was way too strong for Lindsey.

"No."

"How do you know?" Cricket turned on her barstool, so she was facing Lindsey.

"I've never told her anything like that."

"Lindsey, I know you well enough to know that you don't have to say anything when you are in lo—" She stopped before finishing her sentence. "I mean when you really, really like someone. You look at them different than you look at the rest of the world."

Lindsey was surprised. "I do?"

"You do. Is it possible that Sarah figured it out and that's why she's avoiding you?"

Lindsey had no idea. How was she supposed to know if she'd looked at Sarah that way or if Sarah had noticed? And if that was the case, how could she correct it?

"Think that's a possibility?"

"I don't know. I guess anything's possible." Lindsey's phone pinged and her stomach clenched. She pulled it from her pocket.

"Is that from Sarah?" Cricket asked.

Lindsey nodded and read the text. "Busy day. Sorry for the delay in responding." Lindsey set her phone on the bar. "Huh. That's not really a response." She had no idea what to think anymore.

❖

Sarah spent the day way over-thinking. She'd avoided answering Lindsey's text for most of the day. It wasn't that she didn't know what to say. It was that she wanted to avoid her—at least till she figured out her own feelings and what to do about them. That dream had really thrown her, and being exhausted from lack of sleep didn't help. Julie had always reminded her that everything looked different when you were tired. Julie. She missed her. That was one thing she was *sure* of.

She opened her laptop and typed Julie's old email address, double-checking that she did it correctly. The last thing she wanted was for this email to find its way to Lindsey by mistake.

Dear Julie,

I hope you are at peace, wherever you are. Where are you? Why aren't you here with me? I miss you so much, every day and think of you often. I'm struggling with some complicated emotions that I wanted to share with you.

It's been some time since you've been gone, and while I still grieve your loss every day, I have found myself developing feelings for someone else. I feel guilty for even considering the possibility of loving someone else. Not that I'm in love with her, but my feelings seem to grow every time I see her.

I feel like I'm caught in between two worlds, and it's been a real challenge for me to reconcile my love for you with my growing feelings for her. I don't know if it's possible to love two people at once, but I find myself constantly torn between these conflicting emotions. I want to be honest with you, and it's important to me that you know how much I still cherish our time together. You will always hold a special place in my heart, and I will never forget the love we shared.

At the same time, I feel like I'm being pulled in a different direction, and I don't know what to do. I hope you can understand what I'm going through and know how much I still love and miss you every day. I'll always be grateful for the time we had together, and I'll always carry your memory with me.

With all my love,
Sarah

Why was this such a big deal? People moved on with their lives all the time after losing their love. Why did just the thought of it terrify her? She was being stupid, and she knew it, but didn't know what to do about it.

CHAPTER ELEVEN

It had been several days since Lindsey had heard from Sarah. She was tempted to text or call but decided against it. Whatever was going on with her, Lindsey figured it was best to let her work it out on her own. But it was driving her crazy.

She'd had several conversations with Cricket and they both agreed that doing nothing was the best thing to do. Or not do.

Lindsey walked in the door after work and was greeted by Maximus, who seemed to be doing his best to trip her by weaving in and out of her legs more than usual. She stepped around him as carefully as she could.

She opened a can of cat food and added it on top of the dry food in his dish. He pounced on it as if he was starving.

Nothing looked appetizing when she peered in the fridge and she decided that supper could wait, or maybe skipped altogether. In the plant room, she carefully lifted the cups with the fig cuttings to see how they were coming along. In a strange way, seeing them develop roots and leaves gave her comfort. It was as if her grandmother was in the room helping them grow.

She thought back to her childhood and the time she'd spent with her. Up until when she met Cricket, she felt like her grandmother was her only real family. Her mother was too caught up in her own life, and the revolving door of men who came and went, to pay much attention to her. She'd been abandoned by her mother emotionally. She'd been abandoned by her grandmother when she died. She'd been abandoned by Tina when she left without warning, and now, she was feeling abandoned by Sarah. Repeat your traumas much? Apparently. She'd never really thought about it before, but she seemed to draw people into her life—Cricket excluded—that in one way or another left her.

Maybe it was better that Sarah had backed out now, before Lindsey had a chance to get too attached. Who was she kidding? She was already attached and by extension, she was hurt by Sarah's absence.

She lifted one of the cups from the shallow bin. It was warm from sitting on the heat mat under it. She was tempted to put it against her cheek to let the warmth seep into her. The roots were visible along the sides of the cup, and it was just about ready to be up-potted. She checked the rest of the cups and was happy to see they were all progressing nicely. She would need to get some decent potting mix and some two-gallon pots to transplant them.

It was only five thirty. The garden store a few blocks over would still be open. She grabbed her keys and drove to the Garden of Life Shop.

"What can I help you with?" The woman looked to be in her mid-thirties. Her very short brown hair stood at attention on the top of her head.

Lindsey glanced at the woman's name tag. "I need a decent potting mix for some fig cuttings, Ginny."

"Are you just starting them or moving them to a larger pot?"

"Does that make a difference?" Lindsey asked, already knowing the answer. She sometimes liked to test the knowledge of salespeople to see if they knew what they were talking about.

"It does make a difference. You want a potting soil mix if you are moving them and something like coco coir and perlite if you're just starting them."

Good answer. Ginny knew what she was talking about. Lindsey explained what she was doing, and Ginny helped her pick out the best soil and pots. The store wasn't too busy, and they chatted for quite a while about figs and house plants and such. Ginny handed Lindsey a business card, wrote her cell number on the back, and told her to call if she had any questions or problems or *anything else* she might need. Then she winked and Lindsey got the impression that she was flirting with her. Was she? Flirting? Yes. Definitely flirting.

"So, that just happened," she said as she loaded her purchases into her car. She slipped the business card in her pocket. "Maybe calling her wouldn't be a bad idea." Ginny was good for her ego, especially after the crap Tina pulled and now that Sarah seemed to have ghosted her.

She unloaded her purchases, brought them into the plant room, and set about making herself a sandwich for dinner. She broke her own rule, settled down on the couch with her food and turned on the TV.

Her phone pinged with a text, and she pulled it out of her pocket. It was from Sarah. Her stomach did that flip-flop thing that it did whenever she thought about her. She'd gotten used to it by now. Without reading the text, she tossed the phone on the couch next to her and took a bite of her sandwich. Hell, she'd waited almost a week to hear from Sarah so that text and Sarah could just wait for her now. She took another bite. *Damn it.* She picked up the phone and opened the message.

Hi! Sorry I've been out of touch. Can we talk? What are you doing Saturday?

Lindsey hated whenever her mother said they had to talk. It always turned into a lecture, with her mother harping about something or other that Lindsey had supposedly done wrong. That was her first thought when she read Sarah's text. What had she done wrong?

Sure. She responded. *Saturday is open. What time and where?* Saturday was two days away. Lindsey wasn't sure her stomach would settle down between now and then, which pissed her off. Why did Sarah seem to have so much power over her emotions?

How about my house at noon? We can have lunch.

That works. Lindsey willed her stomach to stop acting like an asshole. It didn't listen. She stared at her phone for what seemed like minutes but was probably only seconds. There were no other texts. She threw the remainder of her sandwich into the trash and scolded herself for having such a ridiculous reaction to Sarah's texts.

❖

It was exactly two minutes to twelve when Lindsey pulled into Sarah's driveway. She silently reprimanded herself for the millionth time for her nerves. Sarah answered the door within moments of Lindsey ringing the bell. She pulled her into a hug. Okay. *That's a good sign.* Lindsey's anxiety began to settle down. It was good to see Sarah. Lindsey hadn't realized how much she'd missed her. Or maybe she did.

"What's going on?" Lindsey asked.

"Come on in. Would you like something to drink?"

Lindsey wanted to get right to the heart of the matter and find out what Sarah wanted to talk about. "No, thanks."

Sarah sat on the couch and patted the spot next to her. This was going to be harder than she thought. She'd spent days trying to figure out what to say to make sure she and Lindsey were on the same page. She needed to let Lindsey know that she cared about her but wasn't ready for a relationship. The last thing she wanted to do was hurt Lindsey. She needed to choose her words carefully. "Lindsey," she started.

Lindsey looked at her and Sarah sensed her anxiety. She took her hand and started again. "Lindsey, it's been two years and several months since Julie died. And as you know I had decided it was time to get on with my life. But…" She let the words trail off. *Don't cry. Don't cry. Nope. Not working.* To her horror, she burst into tears.

Lindsey had her arms around her in a split second. "It's okay. I've got you. Let it out."

Why did she have to be so kind? It only made this harder. "I've…" She started again, but her tears weren't stopping. She looked into Lindsey's caring eyes, and without thinking, she leaned into her and kissed her. Hard. Demanding. *This wasn't the plan.* But she found she couldn't stop. It felt good. Incredible. It had been so long.

And Lindsey was kissing her back. Sarah accepted the tongue Lindsey pressed against her lips. Her center was on fire, and she felt a rush of wetness. It was as if she'd been dying of thirst and Lindsey was offering her water. She was determined to drink every last drop. She shut her brain down and let her body take over. Lips. Hands. Bodies pressed together. Clothes were strewn about the floor.

She had trouble catching her breath when it was over. Tears leaked from her eyes and landed on Lindsey's shoulder as she lay on the couch beneath her. Oh shit. What had just happened?

She slipped off Lindsey, sat down on the floor, located her shirt, and slipped it over her head. Embarrassed. Dying inside.

"Hey." Lindsey sat up. "Are you alright?"

Sarah nodded, not sure what to say.

Lindsey sat on the floor next to her and kissed her on the cheek.

Sarah turned her face away. The tears were back in full force. She couldn't seem to stop them.

"Is it Julie?" Sarah could hear the concern in Lindsey's voice.

She nodded again. In her brain she knew what she'd just done was okay. She was single. Julie was gone. But in her heart, it didn't feel right. Her plan to tell Lindsey that they needed to keep things strictly as friends between them had backfired. She had no idea how this had happened. How had she let it happen? Not let it. She was the one who started it.

"Talk to me," Lindsey said.

"I'm sorry."

"Don't be. I'm not. I've wanted that for almost as long as I've known you. I didn't think it was what you wanted."

It *wasn't* what Sarah wanted. She let her physical need get in the way of reason. How could they ever backtrack from this?

"I'm sorry," Sarah repeated.

Lindsey attempted to take Sarah's hand, but Sarah pulled it away. She could see the hurt in Lindsey's eyes.

"What are you sorry for?" Lindsey asked.

"This."

"Making love? Being with me?"

"Yes."

"Why?" Lindsey asked, confused. It was only minutes ago Sarah had her hands and mouth all over her. What had changed in the last two minutes?

Sarah shook her head. That wasn't an answer and Lindsey repeated the question.

"I..."

"You what? Sarah, look at me."

Sarah slowly turned to Lindsey. The crying had stopped, but her cheeks were wet with tears.

Lindsey brushed them away with her thumb. "Please don't be sorry."

"I just needed..."

"It's okay that you needed. You're allowed to have wants and needs."

"And you were here."

Lindsey wasn't sure what she was trying to say.

"I don't want this to happen again. I don't think we should take this any further. I just needed something—something—I don't know."

Lindsey's heart sank. "Are you saying I was just the closest body? Any *body* in the storm would have sufficed?" She suddenly felt used.

Sarah didn't respond.

"Sarah?"

"I can't. Maybe you should go."

Lindsey shook her head. What? They'd just made love and now Sarah wanted her to leave. What the hell?

"Please."

"Sarah."

"Please, Lindsey."

Lindsey scooped up her clothes and slipped them on. She had trouble finding one of her shoes and found it on the other side of the couch, not sure how it had gotten there. Shoes and clothes were flung everywhere in their frenzy.

She stopped at the door and looked back at Sarah still sitting on the floor. She considered saying something—anything—but there wasn't anything left to say. Sarah had asked her to leave. She had no choice.

A plethora of emotions cascaded through her as she slid into the driver's seat. Hurt. Confusion. Anger. Helplessness.

She made it all the way home before her own tears started. She'd been so hopeful when Sarah kissed her and then it went further. It went as far as it could go and then it blew up and Lindsey had no idea why. Or maybe she did. Julie.

If Sarah wasn't ready, then why did she kiss Lindsey? Why did she make love to her? Lindsey wasn't alone on that couch. Sarah was right there with her every step of the way. Until she wasn't.

Maximus met her at the door. "At least you still like me," she said. She wasn't so sure about Sarah. "I didn't even get lunch." She laughed at the stupidity of her thought. She splashed cool water on her face in the kitchen sink.

"What do you think?" she asked the cat. "Did she use me?" It certainly felt that way. "Damn it." She didn't know what to do with herself. She wandered through the house and ended up in her bedroom. She threw herself across the bed and reached for her phone in her pocket to call Cricket. A surge of acid rose up her throat. Panic. Her phone wasn't there. "Oh, dear God. Please don't tell me I left it at Sarah's." It probably fell out of her pocket when her pants ended up on the floor. How the hell was she going to get it back? The last thing she wanted to do was go back to Sarah's house. Not after the way Sarah asked her—told her—to leave. "Shit. Shit. Shit."

What the hell was she supposed to do now? She decided to drive to Cricket's house and hoped she was home. Cricket's car was in the driveway, but that didn't mean she wasn't out with Trevor. Lindsey was relieved when she heard Cricket inside a few moments before she answered the door.

"Hey there. You look like crap." Cricket was nothing if not honest. Sometimes too honest.

"Thanks. Crying will do that." Lindsey followed Cricket into the house.

"Why were you crying?" Cricket poured them each a glass of wine and handed one to Lindsey. It was nice to have a friend who knew you so well and what you needed. They sat across from each other at the kitchen table. Cricket pushed the bottle closer to Lindsey.

Lindsey told her what had happened with Sarah. Her anger was renewed with each detail.

"What did she want to talk to you about in the first place?" Cricket asked.

"No idea. I don't know if she planned for that to happen or what."

"You think she planned to seduce you and then kick you out?" Cricket asked. "From what you've told me, that doesn't sound like her."

"I don't know what to think anymore. I just know it hurt." Lindsey downed half of her wine and refilled her glass.

"Of course it did, honey."

"I'm pretty sure she was feeling guilty about Julie." She shook her head. "Even if that was the case, she should have talked to me about it, not told me to get out."

"No argument from me. That was just cruel." Cricket's phone rang. She glanced at it and hit the end button.

"Was that Trevor? You can take it if you want to." The last thing Lindsey wanted to do was get in the way of Cricket's love life.

"It was and I can call him back later. You've got my attention now."

Lindsey was grateful. "Thank you."

"You don't have to thank me for being your friend."

"I haven't told you the worse part," Lindsey said.

"It gets worse?"

Lindsey laughed despite how miserable she felt. "It's more like the cherry on top. I must have left my phone there."

"Oh, shit."

"Exactly. I don't know what to do about it. I sure as hell can't go back and get it."

"Want me to go get it?" Cricket asked. "Cause, I will, and I'll be happy to give Sarah a piece of my mind."

"You know you don't have too much of your mind to spare," Lindsey said.

Cricket smiled. "Even miserable you still find time to insult me."

"It's only 'cause I love you."

"I love you too. That's why I am willing to give some of my minuscule mind to Sarah for you. What do you think?"

"No. I don't want you to do that. I'm pissed, but I don't want to hurt her."

"After what she just did to you? How about if I just go over there and get your phone and keep my mind intact?"

"I don't know. Let me think about it." She finished her wine and considered refilling her glass again but decided against it. Getting drunk wasn't out of the question, but it would have to wait till she got home. Driving under the influence was not something she ever wanted to do. "Do you have plans with Trevor tonight?"

"I do, but I can cancel them."

"No. I appreciate that. I don't want you to. I'll just live vicariously through you. I've given up on love." Of course, she thought she'd given up on love when Tina left her. She hadn't planned on having feelings for someone else. For Sarah. Look where that got her. Nowhere. That wasn't exactly true. It got her hurt and phoneless. "I'm going to go home, take a long hot bath, and go to bed."

"Um," Cricket said. "It's only three o'clock. That's kind of early to go to bed."

Only three o'clock? How could that be when it felt like she'd already lived a week's worth of emotions? "Good point. I'll go home feed the cat, water my plants, take a bath, and *then* go to bed."

"So, you'll be in bed by five instead of four?" Cricket asked.

"Maybe six. I said my bath was going to be long." Lindsey rubbed her hands together to try to release some of the tension and frustration that had built up inside her.

"What are you going to do about Sarah?" Cricket asked.

"Nothing. What can I do? That friendship is obviously over. Which crushes me by the way."

"I'm so sorry. What can I do to help?"

"You're already doing it. Thank you for being here for me." Lindsey stood. "I'm going to get going. That bath isn't going to take itself."

Cricket walked her to the door. "I'd tell you to call me later, but that's not going to happen. Tell you what, email and let me know how you're doing."

"Emails are what got me into this mess in the first place."

"Do it anyway. I care about you and want to make sure you're alright." Cricket hugged her, adding an extra tight squeeze before releasing her.

"Thanks. Have fun on your date. Tell the good doctor I said hi."

"Will do. Go take your bath, play with your plants, and try to get some sleep. Remember, this too shall pass."

"Like bad gas?"

"Exactly. I love you."

"I love you, too. Thanks," Lindsey replied. She sat in her car for several minutes, trying to figure out what had gone wrong with Sarah. She had no answers.

Once home, she refilled Maximus's food bowl, at his insistence, even though it was nearly full, and filled the bathtub with hot water. She realized as she got undressed that she'd put her underwear on inside out in her haste to leave. None of it made sense to her. She replayed it in her mind, and the only conclusion she came to was that Sarah needed her in the heat of the moment and then was done with her. Thrown away like yesterday's trash. She didn't need people like that in her life. She'd had enough of that when she was growing up. The hell with it and the hell with Sarah. She was so done with her.

She threw a lavender bath bomb into the tub, climbed in, and soaked until the water turned cold. That was also how her heart felt. Cold. Empty. *Thanks for nothing, Sarah.*

CHAPTER TWELVE

S arah couldn't believe what she let happen. What she *made* happen. Her body reacted to the memory of Lindsey's lips on hers—of Lindsey's fingers inside her—of Lindsey, naked underneath her. She sat on the floor for quite a while after Lindsey left. Correction. After she told Lindsey to leave.

When she finally got up and gathered her clothes, she found Lindsey's phone in the tangled mess. *Well, damn. That's not good.* She certainly couldn't call her to tell her to come and get it. And there was no way she could face her, even if she could call her.

Her thoughts bounced from Lindsey to Julie and back again as she put her clothes back on. Julie was gone. She knew that. And now Lindsey was gone too because Sarah had pushed her away. Lindsey must hate her.

What was it she had said? She'd wanted Sarah for almost as long as they'd known each other. So her mother had been right. Lindsey did have feelings for her. At least she did before Sarah acted like an ass and kicked her out. Maybe that was for the best. Not the making love part. That had been a mistake and never should have happened. But it was best that Lindsey was out of her life.

Sarah didn't want Lindsey to have feelings for her and she didn't want to have feelings for Lindsey. But she did, didn't she? There was no getting around that part. It wasn't just sex to her.

Her true feelings came through and she had no control to stop them. That scared her. A lot.

The question was why? Why were her feelings for Lindsey—or anyone other than Julie—so frightening? Some of it was guilt. That was for sure. But the rest? Julie was here one minute and gone the next. Gone in the blink of an eye. No good-bye. No happily ever after. Just gone. How could she give her heart to anyone ever again when life was so unreliable?

She got up and put Lindsey's phone on the library table by the door. She would deal with it tomorrow. Maybe drop it off at Lindsey's house when she was on her lunch break, when she knew Lindsey wouldn't be home. The coward's way out? For sure. But that was all she could muster right now.

She needed to put all her conflicting feelings somewhere, and her latest painting seemed like the most logical place. Upstairs, she put her painting apron on and set to work. Each brush stroke was filled with emotion. Fear. Grief. Surprise. Wonder. Rinse and repeat. She didn't stop until nearly ten o'clock when her stomach protested. She'd missed lunch as well as dinner.

She cleaned her brushes, washed her hands, and made her way down to the kitchen. After deciding on a plate of cheese and crackers—the appetizer she'd put together for her lunch with Lindsey—she settled down with it on the couch in front of the TV. That seemed to be where she ate most of the time since Julie died. Since Julie died. What had she done with her life since Julie died? Not much. And when she decided it was time to live again, she screwed it up. And there was no going back from this. She lost a good friend in the process. She was a mess. Why did she have to give in to her desire? Was it desire? Or was it a need for human connection? And did it even matter?

She got herself ready for bed and slipped under the covers. But sleep eluded her. That seemed to be a recurring theme lately—and Lindsey was the one responsible for it. But Lindsey wasn't to blame for what happened. Sarah was.

❖

Lindsey wasn't sure how she'd gotten though the workday, but she did. Cricket checked on her several times to see how she was doing. You couldn't beat a good friend like that. Lindsey went past her house and continued around the block three times, trying to walk away her frustration, before going home. It didn't help. She was surprised to find a plastic bag stuffed between her screen door and front door, hanging on the doorknob. She grabbed the bag, unlocked the door, and let herself in. Maximus was nowhere to be seen. She found him sleeping in the bay window in the living room, enjoying the sunshine.

After depositing her backpack on the couch, Lindsey looked in the bag. Whatever it was, was wrapped in bubble wrap. Inside the bubble wrap she found her phone. "Well, I'll be damned. I guess this means Sarah's breaking up with me," she said sarcastically. "There goes my plans to propose."

Maximus looked up at her and yawned.

"My thoughts exactly," Lindsey said. "Where did I put that business card from the garden store?" She found it on her dresser. She must have taken it out of her pants pocket before she put them in the laundry hamper.

"Time to move on from that very brief encounter," she said to Maximus, as she passed through the living room on her way to the kitchen. She looked through the freezer for a frozen meal. She was sure there must be at least one left from her recent shopping trip. She found one way in the back underneath a loaf of bread.

She took the cardboard tray out of the box and peeled back the plastic film on one corner. Most of the peas had escaped their confines and were mixed in with the mashed potatoes. "Don't get used to being together," she said to the potatoes. "Those peas are only going to hurt you." She shook her head. "I'm losing my mind, talking to the vegetables. Are potatoes vegetables?" She popped the tray into the microwave and pressed the button for four minutes.

She leaned a hip against the counter and stared at the business card in her hand. Should she or shouldn't she? She wasn't looking for a relationship, but maybe a little fun wouldn't be a bad thing.

Hey there! It's Lindsey the fig lady. How are you doing? She typed on her phone and hit send.

She set the phone on the counter while she waited for the microwave to finish. Her phone pinged with a text a second before the microwave beeped. She ignored the phone, pulled the tray out, stirred the potatoes, trying to push the peas back where they belonged and put it back in for another three minutes.

She read the incoming text. *Hi Lindsey!! What are you doing tonight?*

Was Ginny asking that so they could get together? Lindsey wasn't sure if she was ready for that. She figured they could text for a while, maybe talk on the phone, and get together sometime in the future. She hesitated before answering, wondering if she should say she's busy or not. She decided to tell the truth. *I was planning on up-potting my figs after eating this delicious frozen dinner.*

I get out of work in an hour. Want help with those figs? I can pick up a pizza if that delicious frozen dinner isn't delicious.

"Oh shit. Not what I expected." Ginny obviously didn't waste any time. Lindsey drummed her fingers on the counter. She wasn't sure what to do. She was still reeling from the crap with Sarah. If she had to be honest with herself, being with Sarah had been wonderful—right up to the time it wasn't.

Would getting together with Ginny tonight be good for her or just make her feel worse about Sarah? Oh, what the hell? Why not? *I would love the help and pizza sounds great.*

Wonderful!! Text me your address and let me know what you like on your pizza. I've got to get back to work. Ginny texted.

"I guess we're doing this," Lindsey said. She replied with her address and the word *pepperoni*. The microwave beeped. She pulled the tray of food out and set it on the counter. She didn't want to dispose of it just in case Ginny didn't show up. She wouldn't be the first woman to disappoint Lindsey this week.

As much as she tried to get Sarah out of her mind, she continued to creep in. Yeah, she was mad, and she was hurt. But she was mostly sad. She already missed Sarah and it had only been one day.

If Ginny was serious about helping her with the figs, she wanted to make sure the room was clean. Or better yet, maybe she should bring everything into the kitchen, and they could work on the table. It occurred to her that maybe the offer to help with figs was just a ruse to come over and—and what? Seduce her? Maybe. Would Lindsey let that happen? No way. She'd slept with women she barely knew when she was younger but never found it satisfying. She needed feelings if she was going to have sex with someone. That's why it was so good with Sarah. *Sarah again. Get out of my head. Leave me and my brain alone.* Against her will, her body reacted to the memory of Sarah kissing her, lying on top of her, having her hands and mouth all over her. "Stop," she said out loud.

Maximus jumped up on the counter and rubbed against her arm. She ran a hand over his black fur. "I wasn't talking to you. I was talking to—well, never mind. I talk to myself. I talk to vegetables and now I'm talking to a cat."

He let out a loud meow.

"At least you talk back to me. I think I would freak out if the veggies did." She gently nudged him until he jumped down to the floor. Counters were off limits, and he knew it. He didn't always obey the rules. Lindsey usually forgave him. But some things were easier to forgive than others. Take what Sarah did for example. *Shit.* There she was again, dancing through Lindsey's mind.

It took three trips to the plant room to get the figs cuttings, potting soil, pots, and watering can. Lindsey spread everything out on the table. One of the cuttings wasn't showing as many roots or top growth. She left that one on the heat mat in the plant room. She'd ask Ginny about it when she got there—if she got there. Her faith in women was sorely lacking. It seemed that Cricket was the only one she could really rely on.

She settled down on the couch with her laptop and watched YouTube videos on up-potting fig cuttings while she waited for Ginny. She was on her third video when her doorbell rang. She wasn't sure if she was happy or disappointed that Ginny had actually shown up.

To her surprise it wasn't Ginny. It was a pizza delivery guy. He balanced a large pizza box on his palm. "It's…" He glanced at the receipt taped to the top of the box. "…twenty-five forty-two."

"What?" Lindsey was confused.

"Total, not including the tip is twenty-five dollars and forty-two cents."

"Who ordered this?" Was this Ginny's idea of bringing a pizza?

He looked at the slip again. "Lindsey. Umm. No last name. Is that you? You didn't order this?"

She shook her head. "No. But I'll pay for it. Hold on." She shut the door, so Maximus didn't get out, while she went in search of cash. Luckily, she always had a stash in one of the pockets of her backpack. She did some quick math in her head to figure out a reasonable tip and returned to the door with the money.

The pizza guy was gone, and in his place stood Ginny, now holding the pizza. "Hello there. I was hoping to get here before the pizza and just barely made it." She pointed to the wad of cash in Lindsey's hand. "Is that my tip?" She smiled.

"Umm—no—umm—it was for the pizza," she said, flustered.

Ginny still had her work clothes on, khaki pants, tan shirt and her name tag pinned to her lapel. The mascara and eye liner she wore accentuated her bright blue eyes. She looked younger than she had in the garden store, under the harsh lights. Lindsey wondered just how old she was.

"Guess I got here just in time. I didn't expect you to pay for it."

"Oh." Lindsey was at a loss for words.

"Can I come in?" Ginny held up the box. "I have pizza." She smiled again.

"Oh, shit." Lindsey put her hand over her mouth. She stepped back. "I'm so sorry. Of course. Please, come in."

Ginny stepped in and gave her a one-armed hug. "Where should I put this?" she asked.

"Oh. Yeah." Lindsey was still having trouble gathering her wits. "In the kitchen. This way." Ginny followed her and set the pizza on the counter.

"I see you were serious about up-potting your figs tonight." She laughed.

"Yep. But we don't have to. I can do it tomorrow," Lindsey said.

"I'm just teasing. I would be happy to help. Should we eat first, before this pizza gets cold?"

Lindsey got two plates from the cabinet and ripped a few paper towels off the roll. The pizza was half pepperoni and half anchovies with mushrooms.

"Hope you don't mind," Ginny said. "I got half of what you like and half for me."

"Not at all," Lindsey responded.

She put two pieces of pizza on a plate and handed it to Ginny and got a couple of slices with pepperoni for herself. "Do you mind if we eat in the living room?" Lindsey asked. "I didn't think it through before I brought the fig stuff in here."

"No problem," Ginny said. "That's fine. Lead the way."

Ginny followed Lindsey again, this time into the living room and they sat next to each other on the couch.

"Oh damn. How stupid of me. What would you like to drink?" Why was she so rattled? It wasn't like she hadn't had women in her home before. Of course, it had been a long time—except for Sarah. Why did she have to take up space in Lindsey's head? It was because, despite everything that had happened, Lindsey still had feelings for her. Strong feelings. Especially after they made love. It may have meant nothing to Sarah, but it meant a lot to

Lindsey. She wasn't going to be able to just sweep her feelings for Sarah under the rug with Ginny.

"Lindsey?" Ginny said. "Did you hear me?"

Lindsey realized she'd stood up but was lost in her head for—for God knows how long. "I'm sorry. What?"

"I said anything would be fine."

"Okay. I'll see what I have." She made a quick exit into the kitchen. She was thankful for a couple of minutes alone. She needed to gather her thoughts. This was a stupid idea. She had a total stranger sitting in her living room eating pizza and expecting—who knows what from her.

Sarah. Sarah was the problem. She had feelings for her and no matter what happened, they weren't going to go away with the snap of her fingers. She snapped them, just to be sure. Nope. Still there. She laughed out loud at the craziness of it.

"What's so funny?"

Ginny startled her. Lindsey hadn't realized she'd followed her into the kitchen. "Nothing. Just stupid thoughts swirling in my head."

"Care to share?"

No. Absolutely not. She ignored the question, opened the fridge door, and peered in. "I have ginger ale, root beer, or orange juice." She turned her attention to Ginny. "Any of those sound good to you?"

"Anything. Really. Grab whatever is close."

Lindsey grabbed two cans of ginger ale. She added ice to two glasses and poured soda.

"Thanks," Ginny said when Lindsey handed her one of the glasses. They made their way back to the living room.

"How was your day?" Lindsey asked, trying to break the awkward silence that seemed to be permeating the air.

"Good. Super busy. Everyone is buying stuff to get their gardens ready. Do you grow anything besides the figs?"

"This is my first summer in this house, so I'm hoping to get a small garden going."

"Flowers or veggies?"

"Both. I guess." Lindsey took a bite of her pizza. Chewing slowly, trying to avoid eye contact with Ginny. How did she get into this position? And more importantly, how could she get out of it? Not that Ginny was unpleasant or weird or anything. Although following her into the kitchen and more or less inviting herself over was kind of strange. Forward.

"Don't wait too long to get it going. The last frost date is coming up and we are already running low on a lot of plants," Ginny said. She didn't seem to notice how uncomfortable Lindsey was.

"When is that?" Lindsey asked even though she knew the answer.

They talked about gardening, pizza, and fig trees for the next half hour with plenty of gaps in between. Another serving of pizza later, Lindsey set her empty plate on the coffee table.

"Ready to work on your cuttings?" Ginny asked.

Lindsey didn't really want her helping. It was almost sacred to her, working with cuttings from her grandmother's original fig tree. She knew if she voiced it, she would sound crazy. Her brain was in overdrive trying to come up with a plausible excuse. Lying wasn't out of the question. "I checked the roots again after I brought them into the kitchen. I think they need several more days before I repot them. The roots don't seem strong enough yet."

Ginny stood. "I can check them for you."

Lindsey made no move to get up. "Umm. No. That's okay. I know I'm not an expert by any means, but I'm going to go with my instincts on this."

"Are you sure? It's no problem."

"I'm sure."

Ginny sat back down. "Okay." Crisis averted.

Lindsey rubbed the back of her neck, and tilted her head from side to side, trying to loosen her muscles. They were as tight as a stretched-out rubber band.

"Need a shoulder rub?" Ginny asked. She wasn't shy, that's for sure.

The last thing Lindsey wanted was Ginny touching her. "No. Thanks. I'm starting to get a migraine. I find that nothing but sleeping helps." Okay, that wasn't true. Lindsey wasn't prone to headaches.

"Do you have any Excedrin? I find that helps."

"It makes me sick to my stomach. I haven't found any medications that works, not even the prescription my doctor gave me." More lies. It was so unlike her. But so was inviting a stranger to her house.

"Wow. That sucks. I'm so sorry. Is there anything I can do to help?" She paused. "I've heard that an orgasm can get rid of a headache."

What? Did she actually just say that? The real reason for her visit became glaringly obvious. It wasn't anything Lindsey was interested in. Her thought went back to Cricket's advice after Tina left her. *If you want to get over someone, get under someone else.* She didn't take that advice then and she wasn't going to do it now.

"I think what I need is sleep." She hoped Ginny would take the obvious hint and leave. She didn't.

"I can understand that. Need help getting ready for bed?"

She was either really dense or really intent on getting Lindsey naked. "No."

"Oh. Okay. I thought…" Ginny didn't finish her sentence, but Lindsey was pretty sure what she was going to say.

"I think we are on different pages here," Lindsey said.

"Or maybe not even in the same book."

"Something like that. I appreciate the offer to help with the figs, the pizza, and the company, but I think I'm going to call it a night." She couldn't be any clearer than that.

"Are you sure?" Ginny asked. She made no move to get up.

Lindsey stood, hoping to encourage Ginny to do the same. "I am. I'll walk you out." Lindsey didn't care at this point if she was being rude. She needed Ginny gone.

That apparently did it. Ginny rose and followed Lindsey to the door. "Maybe next time," she said. Without warning—or permission—she kissed Lindsey on the mouth, running her tongue over Lindsey's bottom lip before pulling back. Without another word, she turned and walked to her car.

Lindsey knew the move was meant to entice her. But it repulsed her instead. She closed the door, went into the bathroom, and brushed her teeth. Overkill, she knew, but she needed to remove the sensation and taste of anchovies that Ginny had planted on her lips.

Finding a new garden store was in order. She could never go back to the one Ginny worked at. Anger rose in her. Anger at Ginny for being so forward. Anger at herself for allowing Ginny to come over and for texting her in the first place. And anger at Sarah for making her feel like she needed someone else around to distract her from her feelings.

She cleaned up the pizza mess and loaded the dishwasher. The fig cuttings on the kitchen table were calling her name. She set about filling the pots with soil and carefully extracting the cuttings from the cups that had been their home for the past sixty days. She lovingly placed each one in its own pot and watered them. It was still too cold at night to put them outside, so she lined them up in the bay window. The sun coming in the southern-facing window during the day would provide enough light for now.

She cleaned the stray dirt, rinsed the now empty cups, and put everything in the closet in the plant room. She plopped down on the couch, glad to be alone and admired the small, but developing trees. "What do you think, Grandma?" she said, looking up. "How'd I do? I could use your blessing to help them grow." She shook her head. "I wish you were here with me. I miss you. I feel really messed up right now."

Maximus jumped up on the couch next to her. "Where you been, buddy? Hiding from that crazy Ginny? I should have joined you under the bed. Think she would have tried to drag me out by my feet?"

He looked at her and meowed.

"You're right. She probably would have." She dug her phone out of her pocket and called Cricket.

"Hello?" Cricket answered.

"Hey."

"Lindsey?"

"Who were you expecting?" Lindsey asked.

"How did you get your phone back? I didn't know if it was you or if Sarah still had it."

"It was in a bag hanging on my doorknob when I got home from work."

"That was kind but cowardly. Hey, if you've had your phone since you got home how come you're just calling me now?" Cricket asked.

"Now that is an interesting story." She didn't offer any details, knowing that it would drive Cricket crazy. Hey, she had to find her amusement where she could.

There were several long moments of silence. "Don't be an ass. Tell me the story. Does it involve Sarah?"

"I'm done with Sarah. This story involves Ginny, the garden store lady." She kicked her shoes off and pulled her feet up under her. She waited until Cricket asked her the next question.

"Who in the hell is that? Did you pick someone up? That is so unlike you. Tell me all the juicy details."

"I wouldn't describe it as juicy. It was more like—" She stopped to think of the best word to describe the encounter. "Hmm. It was more like pushy."

"Was she pushy, or were you?"

"Come on now. Have you ever seen me be pushy?"

"No. Will you get on with it. Tell me what happened."

Lindsey told her how she'd met Ginny and how she'd come to be Lindsey's guest.

"You're right. That is an interesting and slightly scary story. You need to stop talking to strangers. The last two almost did you in," Cricket said.

"Two?"

"Ginny and Sarah."

"It started out great with Sarah. I don't think we need to count her." Yes, she was hurt and angry, but her true feelings hadn't changed.

"Did you forget that I was with you after everything happened? I saw how hurt you were. I hated seeing you like that."

Lindsey's first instinct was to defend Sarah, even after what she'd done. She decided against it. It would only make Cricket put Sarah down more. "I appreciate that."

"You need to forget about that woman."

Forget about her? That was far easier said than done.

CHAPTER THIRTEEN

It had been days since the *incident*, as Sarah referred to it in her head. She didn't want to think of it as making love, or worse yet, just sex. She tried not to think about it, because every time she did, her body reacted. Not that the sensations weren't pleasant. They sure as hell were. But it was also guilt-inducing. She couldn't seem to let that go. Guilt, not only because she felt like she'd betrayed Julie, but guilt for how badly she'd treated Lindsey. She could only guess how much she'd hurt her. She was sorry about that. And worse yet, she missed her.

She considered writing a note to put in with Lindsey's phone when she returned it, but after starting it several times she ended up with a pile of crumpled paper that she'd thrown across the room out of frustration. There was no excuse for what she had done, and no apology was good enough. If she was being honest with herself, she was also afraid of opening that door again. She was better off not having Lindsey in her life. And Lindsey was probably better off not seeing Sarah either. It would only cause Lindsey more hurt in the long run.

She was dealing with these swirling emotions alone—just like she'd done with her grief since Julie died. Her family had encouraged her to join a grief support group, but she'd resisted. She didn't want to sit around with a bunch of strangers who were as sad as she had been—maybe still was.

But that one stranger who had come into her life—Lindsey—had made her feel so much better. Maybe strangers could help. Her sister had offered to find her a group to go to. Sarah had no idea if she'd ever found one or not. Only one way to find out.

She called Mary as soon as she got home from work. "Quick question. Did you ever look up support groups?"

"Well, hello to you too," Mary said.

"Hello. Did you?"

"Are you thinking of going?"

Why couldn't she just answer the question? "Yes."

"What changed? I mean you seemed to be doing so much better lately."

Sarah poured Cheerios into a bowl. "I was. Am. I just think I need something more."

"I'm glad you are finally getting help. I've been worried about you. Making a new friend seemed to be a step in the right direction. How is Lindsey doing?"

"Fine." Sarah's heart dropped into her stomach at the mention of Lindsey's name. This wasn't supposed to be a whole discussion. Sarah only wanted the information. "Did you find a group, or should I google it myself?"

"Hold on. I have it here somewhere in the notes on my phone. Hold on," she said again.

"Are you still there?" Sarah asked after what seemed like forever.

"Oh, here it is. I found several, but this seemed to be the closest. They meet...wait."

This was turning into a much too long conversation. Sarah should have just done an internet search herself. "Mary?"

"Yes. Yes. I'm still here. There is a meeting tonight. Soooo." She drew the word out, trying Sarah's patience. "They apparently meet every Wednesday at seven."

"Where is it?"

"It's at the community center on Ridge. I think that's by the old Burger King. Not the new one on Crescent."

"I know where it is. Thanks for the information."

"Of course. Hey, I wanted to invite you and Lindsey to dinner on Friday night if you're both free."

Lindsey again. At some point she needed to tell her family that Lindsey was no longer in her life. But now was not the time. "I'll have to let you know."

"Sure. The sooner the better. I am going grocery shopping tomorrow after work. I know what you like and don't, but can you let me know Lindsey's food preferences? You probably know them already. You two seem pretty close."

"I'll let you know," Sarah repeated, working to keep the irritation out of her voice. "Listen, I'm almost—"

"Do you think you will go to the meeting tonight?" Mary said, cutting her off.

"I'm thinking about it. I'm going to get—"

"Let me know. Okay? I mean, if you go, text me afterward and let me know how it went."

"Sure. I'm about to eat, so I'm going to get going," Sarah said. She hit the end button on her phone before Mary had a chance to respond.

The thought of going to a meeting was intimidating. She needed to swallow her fear and do it anyway. Wasn't that the saying? Something like that.

She looked at the clock on the stove. She had enough time to eat her cereal and change her clothes before the meeting. That is, *if* she decided to go. She hadn't made up her mind yet. To go or not to go. That was the question. What was the answer? She did her best to turn her brain off, knowing full well that she couldn't.

With dinner—she added two pieces of toast to her bowl of cereal—behind her, she changed out of her work clothes and into jeans and a light blue pullover top. She jumped into her car and headed in the direction of the community center, still not a hundred percent sure she would go in.

The parking lot wasn't very full, and she had no trouble finding a spot near the door. It was quarter to seven; she still had time to decide whether to go in or not. A knock on her car window made her jump. She rolled it down a couple of inches.

"Hi. I'm so sorry to bother you. Do you know if this is where the grief support group meets? I'm new in town and have no idea what I'm doing?" She was tall, with long brown hair and light brown eyes—the same color as Lindsey's. *Get out of my head, Lindsey. I don't need you here tonight.*

Sarah pressed the button, sending the window all the way down. "I believe it is. I don't know what room it's in. This is my first time here."

"Oh. Obviously, mine too. Would you mind if we went in together? I'm embarrassed to admit this, but I'm super anxious." She offered a hand through the open window. "I'm Theresa, by the way."

Sarah shook her hand. "Sarah. And I'm nervous too. So, sure, we can go in together." *So, I guess I'm doing this.* She rolled up the window and got out of the car, still unsure if she *wanted* to do it.

Once inside, they found a large posterboard sign on an easel with the words GRIEF SUPPORT GROUP Room 130, and an arrow pointing to the left. They had no trouble finding the room. There was a handful of people milling about. Several large tables were folded and pushed against one wall with folded chairs in a rack in front of them. A dozen or so chairs were arranged in a circle in the center of the room. A small table with snacks and a pitcher of water and paper cups sat off to the side.

"Welcome," a stocky man with a gray beard and a bald head greeted them. "I'm Dan, the facilitator."

They introduced themselves in turn.

"Nice to meet you. Feel free to grab a snack and sit anywhere you'd like. We'll get started soon."

Sarah's stomach objected to eating anything, but her dry mouth thought a glass of water would be a good idea. She made her way over to the table, poured herself a glass, and drank half of it down. She finished it by the time everyone had taken a seat. Theresa patted the seat next to her and Sarah sat.

Dan started the meeting. Almost everyone seemed to know each other, except Sarah and Theresa. "We have a couple of new people tonight. So, let's go around the circle and introduce ourselves. Tell us briefly what brought you here. We'll get more in depth in a bit. I'll start. I'm Dan and I've been the facilitator for this group for two years. I joined my first support group four years ago when both of my parents died within two weeks of each other. I found it quite helpful and decided to start a group to help others."

Each person in turn introduced themselves and said why they were there. The closer it got to Sarah's turn, the more anxious she felt. She rubbed her palms together and took a deep breath. It didn't seem to help.

"I'm Sarah," she said when it was her turn. "My wife, Julie, died more than two years ago. I've been dealing with it pretty much on my own. Until now. I guess. This is my first meeting." She breathed a sigh of relief when the attention moved off her and on to Theresa.

After the introductions—Sarah hoped there wouldn't be a test at the end because she didn't pay close attention to anyone's name, she was too caught up in her own thoughts—Dan asked if there was anything or any particular struggles anyone wanted to share. Sarah was surprised at how many people were willing to share their personal stories. One person's story in particular, caught her attention. It was similar to Sarah's. Her husband died a year and a half ago and she met someone new. They'd gone out a bunch of times and she really liked him but felt so guilty moving on. Like she was betraying her husband.

"I feel the same," Sarah said.

"What did you do about it?" the woman asked. Sarah really wished she had paid better attention to names.

"I stopped seeing her."

"Why?" Dan asked. "Wasn't it going well?"

Sarah wasn't sure how much she wanted to share, and she hesitated.

"Nothing leaves this room, Sarah. This is a safe space," Dan said.

Sarah hated that everyone was looking at her, waiting for an answer. "We didn't really date. I mean we started out as friends, but my feelings got in the way. I thought it was better to stop seeing her altogether."

"I don't want to stop seeing him," the woman said. "I need to figure out how to not feel guilty about it."

"That makes a lot of sense, Gabrielle," Dan said. "Anyone have any input on this or gone through it?"

Gabrielle. Sarah repeated her name several times in her head.

Several people suggested things that Sarah didn't think would be helpful. "Sarah," Dan said. "Tell us more about your experience. Do you feel better since cutting things off with your friend? Were you afraid she wouldn't return your feelings?"

Sarah was surprised to find she actually wanted to share. She was tired of dealing with this alone. "I believe she shared my feelings, and no, I don't feel better. I don't know how I feel. I miss her, I know that."

"Did she want to take it to the next level, and you didn't?"

Sarah had to think about that for a few moments. She was the one who brought it to the *next level*, even though Lindsey was a very willing participant. "I can't see myself having another relationship after losing Julie. I don't know if that was what my friend wanted or not."

"So, you never talked about it with her?" Gabrielle asked.

"No," Sarah responded. "Have you talked to your guy about it?"

"Yes. We've talked. He said he understands. He's exceptionally kind and patient. Do you feel like your friend wouldn't be like that?"

No. Lindsey was one of the kindest people she ever met. And Sarah was sure if she asked her to be patient while Sarah worked out her guilt and her feelings, she would be. "That's not it. She isn't the problem. I am."

"That's how I feel," Gabrielle said. "He hasn't done anything but be there for me."

"How do we get around this guilt and grief?" Sarah asked. Did she even want to? Wallowing in grief seemed to be a way of life for her for so long that it started to seem natural.

"Anyone else been through this?" Dan asked the group.

"I have," the man two seats over said.

"Tell us about it, Steve," Dan said.

"My wife died three years ago. I remarried a year ago. When I first started dating my new wife, I had all the guilt feelings too. I did talk to her about it and like Gabrielle's guy, she was very understanding. She was willing to talk about my first wife and acknowledged how important she'd been to me."

"How did you get over it? The guilt?" Dan asked.

"Time. The more I fell in love with my current wife, the less guilt I felt. It wasn't that my first wife wasn't important anymore. It was more like I knew how great love and a good marriage could be because of her. I knew she loved me and wouldn't want me to live in grief and self-pity forever. She would want me to move on. Don't you think that's what your husband would have wanted for you, Gabrielle? And your wife, Sarah?"

"I haven't thought about it that way," Gabrielle said. "If it was the other way around, I would want him to continue living and be happy."

"Can I ask you why you come to these meetings if your wife died three years ago, and you're happily remarried?" Sarah asked. She wondered if the grief lasted forever.

"Sure," Steve said. "I'm not a regular but, I guess I like to come here every once in a while, to remember what it was like to lose someone and how you can go on. That may sound strange, but it reminds me that life continues if you let it. You can rebuild it when you think there is nothing left to live for. And just because I'm remarried doesn't mean I don't still miss my first wife."

That really hit home for Sarah. She did feel like she'd had nothing left to live for. She'd gone through the motions of living for more than two years without Julie but wasn't really living at all.

"I've had moments where I resented my new guy," Gabrielle said. "Because he is alive, and my husband is dead. Almost as if it was his fault."

Sarah found herself nodding her head. She hadn't realized that she also had moments of feeling that way. How could Lindsey come into her life and be so wonderful when Julie couldn't be here? And if Julie was here, Lindsey wouldn't be in her life. She was mad at them both. Unfair, Sarah knew, but she couldn't help it. She wondered if she should voice it.

"I think that's very normal," Dan said.

"How do you make it stop," Sarah asked.

"You need to acknowledge the feelings and let them pass through you," Dan said. "If you try to fight them, they only intensify."

It sounded good in theory. But the feelings were so hard to feel. "I'm not sure how to do that," Sarah said.

"Surrender to the feelings. When you feel them creeping in, raise your hands and literally think or say 'I surrender these feelings,'" Dan said. "I know it sounds kind of whoo-hoo, but it does work." He held his hands up and looked toward the ceiling to demonstrate.

Sarah hadn't realized just how many feelings were involved in losing Julie and meeting Lindsey. Sadness. Anger. Resentment. Grief. Hope. Hope? Yes, hope. She'd had hope that life could return to somewhat normal after she'd met Lindsey. She missed that feeling almost as much as she missed Lindsey.

"Life needs to go on, Sarah," Steve said. "If I'd resisted a new relationship, I wouldn't have a great wife and marriage right now. We're even talking about having kids. Two years ago I wouldn't have thought that was possible."

"But what about your first wife?" Sarah asked. "Does your new marriage lessen your love or your memories of her?"

"Not at all," Steve responded. "If anything, it strengthens them?"

"I don't understand how that's possible," Sarah said.

"I am honoring the love for my first wife by living my life. If I had curled up in a ball and refused to go on that would have been disrespectful to her."

Had Sarah been disrespectful to Julie's memory the last couple of years? Was she being disrespectful now? She had a lot to think about. Her brain was bouncing from one thought to another as she drove home. She wished she could call Lindsey and talk to her about it, but after the way she treated her, she doubted if Lindsey would ever want to talk to her again. And Sarah couldn't blame her. Calling her and inviting her back into her life wouldn't have been a good idea anyway. That was a can of worms she shouldn't open ever again. The thought made Sarah very sad.

CHAPTER FOURTEEN

S arah had trouble keeping her mind on work the next day. She had a lot to think about. Was she blaming Lindsey for all her confusing feelings? All Lindsey did was be her friend. She'd had feelings for Sarah, but never acted on them or even mentioned them until Sarah kissed her. Lindsey hadn't pushed for anything. She wasn't at fault for any of this, yet Sarah had punished her—banished her. That was on her. And she was sorry.

She sent a text to her sister-in-law, Robin. *What are you doing after work? Any time to get together for a bit?*

It took over an hour for Robin to answer. *Sure. Thomas said he would feed the kids supper. Everything ok?*

Yes. Sarah texted back. *Could use some advice and you're the wisest person I know.*

LOL Flattery will get you everywhere. Should I meet you at your house? Robin texted.

Yes. Please and thank you. I'll be home by 6:20.

Robin responded with a heart and a thumbs up.

Two more hours before she could go home. She took a deep breath and dived back into work, doing her best to keep her mind on the task at hand. She was only semi-successful.

Robin knocked on Sarah's door a half hour after Sarah got home. "Thank you so much for coming." Sarah gave Robin a hug.

"Of course. Happy to be here."

"Too early for wine?" Sarah asked as Robin followed her into the kitchen.

"Never," Robin replied.

Sarah poured two glasses and handed one to Robin. She took her glass along with a plate of cheese and crackers that she'd put together as soon as she got home and led the way to the living room. She set the plate on the coffee table and she and Robin sat on the couch.

"What's going on?" Robin asked.

Sarah wasn't sure where to start. She sipped her wine hoping there was an answer in her glass. There wasn't.

Robin raised her eyebrows, keeping her attention on Sarah. "Whatever it is, you can tell me."

"I know. And I appreciate that. You know Lindsey," she started.

"Of course."

"Well, something happened with her and…" She paused to gather her thoughts. "And well, I felt guilty about it and basically told her to leave." She waited to let that sink in.

"Wait. I think I need more information here. What happened exactly?"

"Sex," Sarah said. "Sex happened. It wasn't anything either one of us planned. It was an accident."

"How do you accidently have sex?"

Sarah laughed at how ludicrous it sounded. "Damned if I know. The point is I was developing feelings for her and felt guilty about it. I invited her over."

"To tell her how you felt?"

"Hell no. Quite the opposite. I was going to make sure that she knew we could never be more than friends." Sarah took a large sip of her wine. This was harder than she thought it would be.

"So let me get this straight. You had feelings but didn't tell her. Why would you need to tell her you could only be friends if she didn't know about your feelings? I'm confused," Robin said.

"Because Mom said she thought Lindsey had feelings for me."

"How would your mother know that and you didn't?"

"I guess I was oblivious. She said she could tell by the way Lindsey looked at me."

"She is pretty good at that sort of thing," Robin said. "She knew I was in love with Thomas before I did. At least that's what she told me after we were engaged. Sorry. This isn't about me. Go on."

"I wanted to make sure that Lindsey knew nothing could happen between us."

"But if you both feel the same, why couldn't you pursue it? And where does the sex part come in?"

"Because of Julie."

Robin put her hand on Sarah's arm. "Julie's gone, honey. That shouldn't stop you from living your life. Don't you think Julie would want you to love again? To live again?"

Sarah didn't even have to think about it. Of course, she would. She nodded.

"Then why would you hesitate at a second chance at love? If it's that obvious how Lindsey feels about you and you feel the same, why wouldn't you jump at it? How do you really feel about her?"

"I…"

"Sarah, just say it. I know you well enough to know that you have analyzed the hell out of this. You've thought of every possible way this could go and how you would feel about it. You said you have feelings for her. I'm just asking you to say it out loud exactly what they are."

Sarah brought her eyes up to Robin's. There was no use denying it. "Okay. I think I love her. Is that what you want to hear?"

"It's what I want *you* to hear," Robin said. "I want you to hear your own words and realize what they mean."

"They mean I leave Julie behind. They mean she's gone forever."

Sarah put her head in her hands. She was exhausted from the arguments in her own head over the last several days.

"Sarah, look at me."

Sarah brought her head up, wiped a stray tear from the corner of her eye, and put her attention on her sister-in-law.

"Julie is the one that left *you* behind. I know she didn't want to, but she did. And, honey, it is forever. At least in this lifetime. You aren't being disloyal to her by loving someone else. You are honoring her memory and the love you shared with her."

Was that true? Was moving on with someone else honoring Julie? Maybe. That's how it was for Steve from the support group.

"If you were the one who died," Robin continued, "would you want Julie to cut herself off from really living, or would you want her to go on and be happy?"

She would want only the best for Julie. And Julie would want the same for her. "I feel like I'm betraying my wife by even thinking about being with someone else," she said. Tears streamed down her face.

"I can understand that. But you're not, Sarah. Not even a little bit." Robin tilted her head. "Where does the sex part come in? You said you were going to tell her nothing could happen and then it did?"

Sarah explained the best she could what had happened. "And then I told her she should leave."

"What? Why?"

"At the time it seemed like the only thing I could do. I felt so guilty after what we'd done."

"How did you feel during?" Robin asked.

Sarah thought back and her body reacted again. "Wonderful."

"And what does that tell you?"

"That I'm a fool." She swiped at the tears on her cheeks.

"You aren't. What I think you are is scared," Robin said.

"Scared?"

"Scared to love and give yourself to someone because the last time you did you lost her. And that hurt. Hurt like hell. I know. But, Sarah, life moves forward. We all have to do it, no matter how scary it seems."

"After what I did, I doubt Lindsey would even talk to me again."

"You won't know unless you try. She may forgive you. She seemed like an understanding person. But I think you need to do some forgiving too."

Sarah was confused. "What?"

"You need to forgive Julie for leaving you." Robin paused. "And you need to forgive yourself for what happened with Lindsey and for your feelings."

Sarah thought about that for several long moments. She sipped her wine while the thoughts jumped around her brain. "You're right. I have been very angry at both of us." She put her hands in the air, closed her eyes, and lifted her chin. She felt the anger and let it pass through her. "I surrender," she said. To her surprise it did seem to help.

She found Robin looking at her when she opened her eyes.

"What was that?" Robin asked.

"Something I learned at a grief support meeting last night."

Robin looked surprised. "You went to a meeting? Was it the first time?"

"Yes and yes."

"Did it help?"

"It got me thinking, which is why I needed to talk to someone who could help me figure things out."

"And you thought of me? I'm flattered."

"I thought of Oprah first, but she didn't return my call."

Robin swatted at her. "Jerk."

"Is that what I've been? A jerk?" Sarah finished her wine and wished she'd brought the bottle into the living room with them.

"Not at all. You've been dealing with a lot of pain. And I think you're doing great. You're starting to take steps in the right direction."

"You think Lindsey is a step in the right direction?" Sarah stood. "Hold that thought. Be right back." She needed more wine for this conversation and retrieved the bottle. She refilled her glass and noticed that Robin hadn't even touched hers. *Oh well. More for me. And I need it.* "So," she said after sitting again. "Lindsey?"

"I don't think that question is for me," Robin said.

Sarah looked around. "I don't see anyone else here."

"You're the one who needs to answer that question. You know how you feel. You know how she feels, or at least you think you do. Only you can decide if you want to try to move forward with it."

"And if I decide that's what I should do, and Lindsey doesn't want to?"

"You won't know unless you talk to her. And I would suggest you actually talk this time and don't end up having accidental sex."

"Am I ever going to live that down?" Sarah asked.

"Probably not. Listen, Sarah, think about it. Decide what you want to do and move forward with it, whether it involves Lindsey or not. You deserve to live a good, full life. Only you can decide what that includes."

"All I've been doing is thinking. I'm driving myself crazy."

"I would suggest you narrow down your thoughts and try to decide one thing at a time. For example, start with what you want to do about Lindsey. I know this sounds harsh, but take Julie out of the equation. This is about you and Lindsey only. If you feel guilty, ignore it, or better yet, do that surrender thing you did and leave it at that." Robin made it sound so easy.

"Break it down into bite-size pieces?"

"Exactly. I have total faith in you that you can handle this. Look how much you've handled already. I know you've had a lot of pain. I think it's time for some happiness. You deserve it, Sarah."

Sarah sipped her wine while she let Robin's words sink in. Did she deserve it? Maybe. Probably. She needed to get her brain, as well as her heart, onboard. She needed to turn that *probably* into a yes. The question was how.

❖

Sarah replayed the conversation with Robin on a continual loop in her head for several days. She needed to talk to Lindsey and see if she could earn her forgiveness and make it right with her. An apology was the first step. It might be the only step if Lindsey wouldn't forgive her. After that, she didn't know.

She woke up early on Saturday after a night of repetitive dreams that involved Lindsey and the possibility of them dating. They started out the same, but each ended differently. She woke up in a cold sweat from one where Lindsey told her she hated her and ordered her out of her house.

That was pretty much what she had done to Lindsey. She initiated sex and then ordered Lindsey to leave. She couldn't blame Lindsey if she did the same—minus the sex part.

Sarah knew that the longer she put off contacting Lindsey, the harder it would be. And the less likely Lindsey would be to forgive her. Too much time had passed already. She wasn't sure if she should call Lindsey or go to her house and talk to her in person—if Lindsey would even let her in. She was still bouncing the question around in her brain as she showered and dressed. She'd made up her mind by the time she finished her second cup of coffee. She was going to go talk to Lindsey in person.

She changed her top from an old T-shirt to a nice button-down blouse and examined herself in the full-length mirror attached to her closet door. After deciding she looked acceptable, she brushed her teeth for the second time that morning and forced herself to get into her car. Her heart felt like it was going to escape her chest and run away in terror as she pulled into Lindsey's driveway. Lindsey's car was parked in front of the house. That was a good sign, but also increased Sarah's anxiety. She closed her eyes, took a deep breath, raised her arms, and surrendered up her nervousness.

It was a full five minutes before she worked up enough courage to walk to the door and ring the bell. She could tell from the look on Lindsey's face when she answered the door that she was surprised—maybe shocked would be a better word—to see Sarah standing there.

"Can I come in?" Sarah asked.

It took several long seconds for Lindsey to step aside to let her pass.

Sarah made her way to the living room. "Thank you for not punching me in the face," Sarah said.

Lindsey didn't know if she was trying to be funny or not. What the hell? The last person Lindsey had expected to see on her porch was Sarah. Acid rose in her throat and settled back down to her stomach, where it threatened to burn a hole clear through her.

"Can I sit down? I would like to talk," Sarah said.

Lindsey shrugged. *This should be interesting.*

Sarah sat on the couch and motioned for Lindsey to sit, and she waited until she did. "First, I want to apologize. I was wrong for asking you to leave after—well, after what happened."

"Okay," Lindsey said.

"I was scared. I felt like I'd just betrayed Julie. The truth is…" She stopped.

"*What* is the truth?" Lindsey asked. She had no idea where Sarah was going with this.

"I was developing feelings for you and I—this is really hard for me," Sarah said. "I'm sorry." She put her hand up. "I'm getting to the point." She paused again and swallowed.

She was developing feelings? That was an unexpected revelation. *And she kicked me out because of them?* That made no sense.

"I had a lot of emotions that I wasn't able to deal with, around both you and Julie. I'm sorry. I'm not explaining this very well."

"Stop saying you're sorry and just tell me what you're talking about" Lindsey was starting to lose patience.

Sarah cleared her throat and started again. "I liked you. I mean I *do* like you. *Really* like you. And I was afraid of that. I felt guilty for it and when I thought you were developing feelings for me as well, that just set off full-blown panic. I was going to tell you that nothing could ever happen between us. And I started to cry, and you put your arms around me, and well—"

"I remember. I was there," Lindsey said bitterly.

"I know you were. My body took over and what happened *happened.*"

"So, it was just your body? You needed a quick lay and I happened to be in close proximity?" She didn't care if it sounded harsh.

Sarah shook her head. "No. No. That wasn't it at all. I had no intention of that happening. And it wouldn't have if it weren't for the feelings I have for you."

"What does that mean?"

"It means it's what I wanted but I felt guilty for wanting it and for acting on it."

"Why can't you say what it was? Making love? Sex? Getting it on? What should we call it?" Lindsey said sarcastically.

"All of the above. I never meant to hurt you."

"You did."

"I know and all I can do is ask your forgiveness," Sarah said.

"You're here so I'll forgive you? You're forgiven. I guess we're done here." She stood. She wasn't sure she wanted to hear anymore.

"No. No. I know I'm not explaining this very well. Please sit. Give me a chance to say this."

Lindsey sat and took a deep breath and waited while Sarah seemed to gather her thoughts. Lindsey wished she'd hurried up with it.

"I miss you. I want you back in my life—in whatever way you want."

In whatever way she wanted? What did that mean? This conversation was bringing up more questions than it was answering.

"Can you say something?" Sarah asked.

"I'm not sure what you want me to say. You're scared. You feel guilty. Yet you want me back in your life? As what? A friend? I'm not sure I trust you anymore."

Sarah leaned forward. "I don't blame you for that. I was an ass. I fully admit that. But that's not who I am. I was running from you because I wanted you. Wanted more than just friendship from you."

"More?" Lindsey needed Sarah to spell it out. Tell her exactly what she meant.

"You made me feel alive again. But in a way it hurt to feel alive when Julie is dead. It felt unfair."

"Unfair to who?"

"Unfair to Julie," Sarah said. Her eyes filled with tears.

There was no way in hell Lindsey was going to offer her any comfort, not after what happened the last time she did. "So, you think because Julie's dead, you should be too. Or at least act like your dead—not really living?"

Sarah seemed to ponder that for several long moments. "In a way, yes. I know that sounds stupid. It sounds stupid even to me, now that I'm saying it out loud. But I have been hurting for so long that feeling good made me feel bad. What I'm trying to say is I'm sorry and I would like to start again. If friends is all you want to be, then I'm good with that." She paused. "But if you would like more—like to see where this could go—then I would like that too."

Wait. What? Was Sarah really saying what Lindsey seemed to be hearing? And if she was, did Lindsey want that? She knew she liked Sarah. But that was before. Before Sarah did what she did. She wasn't sure she could trust her. She'd been hurt in the past. She trusted Tina and she ripped Lindsey's heart to shreds.

And just when it was fully healed, Sarah stuck a knife in it and twisted.

And here she was, sitting in Lindsey's living room saying she wanted to be more than friends. Is that what Lindsey had just heard? She needed to be sure. "What exactly are you saying?"

Sarah sucked a breath in and blew it out. "I want to be with you. I want to date—do they still call it that?" Her laugh sounded nervous. "I want to see what you and I can be together."

Lindsey didn't respond. If Sarah had said this two weeks ago, she would have jumped at the chance. Now she wasn't sure.

"Can you say something?" Sarah said after several long minutes of silence. "Please."

"I have nothing to say right now. I need to think about this." There was no easy answer to this one. Once the trust was broken could you get it back? Lindsey didn't know.

"Yes. Yes. Of course. I'm so sorry, Lindsey. Please believe me."

Lindsey expected Sarah to get up at that point and leave, but she made no moves to do so. Lindsey didn't want to kick her out. She knew firsthand how awful that could make you feel. She thought maybe if she sat there and didn't say anything, Sarah would get the message and leave on her own. The strategy worked. Sarah left a few minutes later, leaving Lindsey wondering what the hell had just happened.

CHAPTER FIFTEEN

I think I blew it. Sarah put the car in reverse and pulled out onto the street. Her nerves had gotten the better of her. She had practiced what she wanted to say a thousand times in her head, but stumbled all over it when she was face-to-face with Lindsey.

Lindsey. It was so good seeing her, even with that stoic look on her face. All she could do now was wait and hope. Hope Lindsey would forgive her and give her a chance. Give them a chance. Oh, how her thoughts had changed in the past few days. Talking to Robin had really helped her see things more clearly.

Whether Lindsey gave them a chance or not, Sarah was prepared to face life full-on again. She thought she'd started that already, but until she accepted her feelings for Lindsey she hadn't really. She was ready now. When you'd loved as deeply as she'd loved Julie, you felt deeply. Felt the love. Felt the pain. Felt the possibility in new beginnings. For the first time in a long time, she knew without a doubt she was ready for that new beginning. She hoped it would be with Lindsey by her side.

She needed to write one final letter to Julie. Once home, she bypassed her laptop and opted for a pen and legal pad, which she found in her desk drawer. She sat at the kitchen table and wrote.

Dear Julie,
I don't know if you can see this, or if you're still here with me in some way. But I have to believe that you are. Or maybe I just choose to believe it.

This is the last time I'll write to you, Julie. I need to move on with my life. I've met someone, and I can't keep living in the past. I don't know where it will go with Lindsey, but I'd like the chance to find out. I hope that's what you would want for me and can understand. I will always love you. You were my soulmate, my partner, my everything. You made me feel alive in a way that no one else ever had. I will cherish our memories together forever, and I will always hold you in my heart. That part will never change.

But I need to live my own life now. I need to see where this new journey takes me. I hope you can forgive me for moving on, but I can't stay stuck in the past forever. I need to keep moving forward. I know that one day we will be together again, Julie. I have got to believe that, because otherwise, the thought of never seeing you again would be too much to bear.

For now, I have to say good-bye. Thank you for everything you gave me, Julie. Thank you for the love, the laughter, the memories. You will always be a part of me, and I will never forget you. Good-bye for now, my love.

Always,
Sarah

She ripped the sheet off the pad, folded it in half, and went in search of a lighter. She found one in the junk drawer. Outside she uncovered the fire pit that she hadn't used in years. Julie was the one who wanted it, and Sarah had been surprised at how much she enjoyed it, especially when they had friends over for the evening. That seemed like forever ago.

She kissed the folded paper, held it over the fire pit, and lit it. It glowed bright yellow and red as the heat built. She released it into the container before the flames reached her fingers and watched as it turned into ash. It was her final gift to Julie, at least in this realm. It was offered up with all the love Sarah had in her heart for her wife. The gesture was meant to release the past and open her heart up to the future. A future Sarah was looking forward to.

❖

Lindsey called Cricket, suspecting she was probably spending the day with Trevor. She was surprised when she answered. "Hey, girl."

"Are you with Trevor?" Lindsey asked. She didn't want to interrupt.

"Not till later. What's going on?"

Lindsey paced back and forth across the living room. "Sarah was here."

"She was?" The surprise in Cricket's voice was evident. "And?"

"And she apologized for what happened."

"For the sex?"

Lindsey thought back to the conversation. "No. For the way she treated me afterward. She said she was scared."

"Scared of what? Scared of you?"

Lindsey made another trek across the room. "Scared of her feelings for me."

"She has feelings for you?" Cricket asked.

"Yes."

"Lindsey, this is like pulling teeth. Can you just tell me what happened and not break it up into bits and pieces?"

Lindsey gave her the gist of the conversation and waited for Cricket's response. "Well?" Lindsey said when one didn't come right away.

"I didn't see that coming. What are your thoughts? I mean, I know you liked her. How do you feel now?"

Lindsey plopped down on the couch. "I still like her. My feelings didn't just disappear because she acted like a jerk. But I don't know. How can I be sure I can trust her after what happened?"

"That, my friend is a good question. I don't think you can know for sure unless you give her a chance. Maybe keep it as friends until you know."

That wasn't a bad idea. Keep it light, friendly, observe things for a while. She didn't want to jump into anything serious. Not with Sarah. Not with anyone. Not right now anyway. She needed to keep her heart wrapped in cellophane, inside a box, in the back of her closet. Way back. It had been through too much in the last year.

"What do you think?" Cricket asked.

"Probably the best idea."

"Just don't get caught up in your feelings and let things happen again."

She didn't need a reminder on that one. No way would anything happen between them until Lindsey was sure of Sarah's feelings and what she was going to do with them. "No chance of that," Lindsey said.

"Listen to me," Cricket said. "Don't get caught up in your feelings."

"You already said that."

"And I might say it again. I know you. You wear your heart on your sleeve."

"Not this time. I've packed it away, where the rust and the moths can't get it."

"Un-huh. Okay. I've got to get ready. You gonna be okay?"

"Good as gold. Right as rain. Hunky-dory. Bright-eyed and bushy-tailed. And any other cliché you want to throw in."

Cricket laughed. "I don't think that last one fits, but whatever."

"Hey, listen," Lindsey said. "You have fun tonight but don't get caught up in your feelings."

"Way too late for that. Call me if you need me. But to be honest, I hope you don't need me."

"I always need you. But I won't call you tonight. Seriously, I hope you have a great time."

"Thanks," Cricket said. "Love you."

"Love you too. Bye."

Lindsey didn't know what she would do without Cricket. Probably curl up in a ball on the floor and suck her thumb.

She had a lot to think about. Sarah had dumped a lot on her, and she was going to sit with it for a few days. Their friendship had blossomed at warp speed. If a relationship was in their future, she couldn't let it happen that way. If she let it happen at all.

Lindsey let a week go by before she contacted Sarah. She'd thought a lot about what she wanted to say. *Hi. I'm willing to try friendship again. If it goes beyond that we need to go slow. But I don't want to even plan that right now.* She hit send.

It took several minutes for a text to come back. *I can handle that. I am grateful for a second chance.*

Would you like to get together sometime? Lindsey texted.

Absolutely. Did you have something in mind?

Lindsey hadn't thought that far ahead. She gave it a few minutes before she answered. *Want to go for a walk on the canal?*

Sarah answered immediately. *Yes! When?*

Tomorrow. Noon. Meet me behind the ice cream shop?

Sarah typed *Great. See you then.* She added a heart emoji and then deleted it. She didn't want to push or give Lindsey the wrong idea.

Sarah woke early the next day. She'd spent the last week hoping and praying that she would hear from Lindsey and was elated that she finally did. It was a great first step. She hoped they could take many more. She knew she needed to play it cool. How different her thoughts and wants were from even a few weeks ago. The fear and guilt were gone—mostly. But she could deal with the bits that remained. Using that surrender trick helped. So did going to another support meeting. She wished she hadn't resisted for so long.

She took a quick shower and sat on the back deck with the Sunday newspaper and cup of coffee. The morning seemed to drag until it was finally time to meet Lindsey.

The weather was perfect for a walk outside. She grabbed a light jacket on her way out the door in case it was cooler by the water. She recognized Lindsey's car as she parked by the ice cream shop. Lindsey wasn't in it.

Sarah tied her jacket around her waist and went in search of her. She found her sitting on a bench by the water. "Hi," she said timidly.

"Hi," Lindsey replied. She made no move to get up, so Sarah sat next to her, leaving a respectable amount of space between them.

"How are you?" Sarah asked.

"I'm okay. You?"

It all felt too formal. "Good." There were several minutes of uncomfortable silence and Sarah wasn't sure Lindsey was truly open to friendship.

"Would you like an ice cream cone?" Sarah asked. "My treat."

Lindsey smiled and for a moment Sarah thought everything would be okay. "Sure. As long as you're buying."

"I am, so get whatever. Eight scoops if that's what you want."

"I want ice cream. Not a stomachache. I think I'll stick with one. Maybe two."

Sarah got up, resisting the urge to take Lindsey's hand. "Come on then. That ice cream is calling our names." The hope rose in Sarah as they made their way around the front of the shop and ordered their ice cream. They each got two scoops of chunky chocolate.

"Thanks," Lindsey said. "I haven't had ice cream since…" Lindsey paused. "Yesterday. I had ice cream for dinner. Don't tell Cricket. She'd yell at me. No, wait. She yells at me when I eat salad."

Sarah laughed, glad they seemed to be back on the road to friendship. "Why?"

"She says no one really likes salad. Which is probably true."

Sarah paid for the ice cream, and they started down the trail on the side of the Erie Canal. They were quiet as they ate and strolled along the paved path. It was a warm day, and Sarah raised her face to the sun. She felt a renewed hope for life and what it could hold for her—for them. Hopefully.

"What are you thinking?" Lindsey asked.

The question took Sarah by surprise. "Just happy to be here. In the sunshine. With you."

Lindsey nodded. If she was being honest with herself, she was happy to be with Sarah too. As much hurt as Sarah had caused her, the feelings she had for her hadn't diminished. She licked the side of her cone to catch a drip of ice cream.

She knew she needed to guard her heart. She could easily give it away to Sarah and have it ripped out of her chest again. She couldn't stand another heartbreak like that. Treading lightly was the only smart thing to do. She hoped she could stick to that. She looked over at Sarah, her straight blond hair pulled back into a ponytail glowed in the bright sunshine. Her deep green eyes held a spark that Lindsey had never seen in another person. The initial edge of sadness that had inhabited them when they first met was gone. Her face, although beautiful then, was even more so. More relaxed. More alive.

Yes. Her heart was in danger with this one. She knew that as well as she knew her own name.

"My turn," Sarah said. "What are you thinking? I can't quite read the look on your face."

"You're reading my face? I can recommend a few books that would probably be more interesting."

"I doubt that."

"That I know books?" Lindsey asked.

"That they would be more interesting than your face." Sarah paused. "Sorry. Too much. I know." She put her hands up. "This is me backing off."

Lindsey looked down and kicked at a small stone. She wasn't sure she wanted Sarah to back off. And that was scary. They'd been together less than an hour and her feelings were right there at the surface again. She did her best to tuck them to the back of her mind. The back of her heart.

They continued for a while in silence. Comfortable silence. It was a perfect day. Sunshine. Birds singing. Perfect company. Lindsey was content.

"Look," Sarah whispered. She halted and took Lindsey's arm to stop her.

About twenty feet in front of them was a mother deer with her fawn. They stood still. Silent. Taking in the beauty of it. The day couldn't get more perfect.

The fawn wandered back into the woods, with its mother close behind. "That was so cool," Sarah said.

Lindsey agreed. "What made you change your mind?" It was a question that Lindsey had thought about but didn't plan on asking.

"About you?"

Lindsey nodded. "Yes. And about possibilities."

Sarah seemed to think about it. "I went to a grief support group, and I talked to my sister-in-law, Robin. I think she opened my eyes to a few things. It helped me let go of Julie." She paused.

Lindsey was surprised. "You let go of Julie?"

"That's not the right way to say it." She sighed. "I guess I accepted that Julie is gone and I'm still here. I made the decision to live. Really live. I mean, I thought I had made the decision before this, but I wasn't truly prepared to move on."

"And you are now?"

Sarah nodded. "Yeah. I thought moving on would mean I didn't really love Julie, or that I was saying she hadn't been that important to me."

Lindsey had no idea how deep these feelings had been for Sarah. It made a lot of sense why she had reacted the way she had.

"But the possibility of allowing myself to love someone else means that what I had with Julie *was* real. It's not that someone else will take her place. It means someone else can be a new addition. It doesn't subtract anything from me or her or my life." She laughed. "I didn't realize this would turn into a discussion about math."

Lindsey smiled. "I'm glad you can share this with me."

"You understand what I'm trying to say?" Sarah asked.

"I do."

"I know my capacity to love. It didn't die with Julie. It was just dormant."

Sarah was drawing Lindsey in deeper with her words. "You think you can love like that again?"

"Absolutely. I don't think it was that I didn't think I could. It was that I didn't want to. I didn't want to love anyone but Julie. I can still love Julie, even though she isn't here. But there isn't a cap—a limit—to my love. I think the more you love, the larger your capacity to do so."

All Lindsey wanted to do in that moment was open her heart to Sarah. To hand it over willingly and let her do whatever she wanted with it. But Cricket's words echoed in her head. *Don't get caught up in your feelings.* She wanted to tell the echo to shut up, but knew it was wiser to listen. She still needed Sarah to prove herself. Prove that she wasn't going to hurt Lindsey again. But this was a great first step.

CHAPTER SIXTEEN

It was a beautiful day, not too hot with super low humidity, and Sarah took advantage of it by going for a walk on her lunch hour. She left the lunch she'd packed in the mini fridge in her office and opted for a hot dog from the street vendor that parked on the sidewalk in front of the building. She pumped on a bit of mustard and continued on her journey, stopping at the park down the street.

She used a napkin to brush a few dry leaves off an old metal bench and sat down. She took in the sounds and sights around her, birds chirping, a woman with a toddler in a stroller, an elderly man walking a dog. It was good to be alive. It had been a long time since she'd felt that way, and there were times she thought she'd never feel that way again.

Her phone rang and for a moment she considered not answering it. She dug it out of her pocket and was surprised to see it was Lindsey calling.

"Hey there," she said.

"Hi. I hope I'm not interrupting your work, but I thought maybe you would be on your lunch hour."

"Your timing is perfect."

"Oh good. Dinner at my house, tonight?" Lindsey said. "I know it's last minute. Cricket and her boyfriend will be there."

"Sure," Sarah responded. "What time and what can I bring?" The thought of meeting Lindsey's best friend was a little intimidating. Sarah was sure Lindsey had told her what happened and how Sarah had acted. She must have thought Sarah was a total jerk.

"Six thirty. And just bring yourself. I've got everything covered. Or better yet, come straight from work, whatever time that is. It will give us some time before everyone else gets here."

They'd talked on the phone and texted several times since their walk on the canal but hadn't seen each other the last several days. Sarah was grateful for the opportunity to see Lindsey again—even if it included her friends. "Sure. That sounds good."

"Excellent. I won't keep you. See you soon."

Sarah said good-bye. One more thing to be grateful for—Lindsey forgave her. She wasn't sure that would have been possible. She hoped they could take it beyond friendship, but if they never did, she would settle for that. She just wanted Lindsey in her life in whatever form that took.

With the workday behind her, Sarah found herself standing at Lindsey's door, ringing the bell. "Hello there," Sarah said when Lindsey answered.

"You look nice." Lindsey pulled Sarah into a hug.

"Just my work clothes," Sarah responded.

"Take the compliment," Lindsey said. "Come on in. I'm getting dinner ready."

"I'll help." Sarah followed Lindsey into the kitchen.

"I would appreciate that. Grab an apron. They're hanging on the hook in the pantry. Grab whichever one you want. You can chop the onions."

Sarah slipped the apron over her head and tied it in the back. "Are you trying to make me cry?"

"Over an apron?"

"Over the onions."

Lindsey laughed. Sarah loved the sound of it. "Don't you know any tricks to stop the tears?"

"None that have ever worked." She watched as Lindsey wet a paper towel and placed it on the cutting board next to a peeled onion.

"What is that supposed to do?" Sarah asked. "Is it to wipe the tears?"

"Nope." Lindsey handed her a sharp knife. "The vapors of the onions are attracted to moisture. That's why they go to the eyes. The paper towel gives them something else to go to."

"Are you kidding?"

"It's for real. Try it." Lindsey filled a pot with water from the sink.

Sarah shook her head, sure that there would be tears streaming down her face within a minute or two. "How big do you want the pieces?"

"Just a rough chop is good," Lindsey said. She set the pan of water on the stove.

Sarah made quick work of the onion, cutting it the way her mother had taught her when she was young. "All done."

"And the tears?" Lindsey asked.

"Oh my God. There aren't any. You were right. I can't believe it."

"You can believe what I tell you."

"I hope you can believe me, too," Sarah said.

"Working on it. I'll get there."

I hope so. "What else can I help with?"

"Hmm. Nothing. I think everything else is under control. Sit, keep me company while I work."

"I've been sitting all day. Give me something to do." It felt good to be doing normal things with Lindsey, working side by side. Just spending time with her.

"Umm. Okay. There's a large pan in the bottom cabinet over there." She pointed. "You can sauté the onion and the garlic. The oil's to the right of the stove."

They were just about done with dinner when Cricket and her boyfriend arrived. Lindsey did the introductions.

"So nice to finally meet you," Cricket said.

"You too," Sarah replied.

"Cricket, would you and Sarah mind setting the dining room table? That will give me a chance to talk to the good doctor here."

"Please call me Trevor," he said.

Sarah got the impression that Lindsey hadn't met him before.

"Sure," Cricket said. She obviously knew her way around Lindsey's kitchen. She handed Sarah dinner and salad plates and piled silverware on top. Sarah carefully carried it all into the dining room and set it on the table. Cricket followed her with wine glasses perched between her fingers and water glasses tucked under her arms.

"You must have been a waitress," Sarah said.

"Nope. Just a big extended family. We were all expected to help when we were together. I learned to get things done as quickly as possible so I could go play with my cousins."

"Good training ground."

Cricket turned her head looking toward the kitchen. Sarah followed her gaze. Lindsey was at the stove stirring a pot of spaghetti sauce talking to Trevor.

Cricket turned her attention back to Sarah. "Please don't take this the wrong way, but I really care about Lindsey."

Sarah braced herself for a tongue-lashing. "I do, too." She hoped she didn't sound too defensive.

"I don't want to see her hurt. Again."

Sarah wasn't sure if she was referring to the hurt caused by Tina or the hurt she'd caused. And she wasn't about to ask.

"So, please tread lightly. Don't give her false hope if there isn't any."

"I'm not doing that. I know I acted poorly in the past, but I've explained that to her. I believe she understands." She wasn't sure what else to say.

"Poorly is an understatement. She was a mess after what happened. Sarah, I do believe you care about her. But you need to know for sure what you want, and if it's Lindsey, you need to treat her right. If it's not, you need to cut her loose before she gets too involved. What happened with Tina took her a long time to get over. She can't take another heartbreak."

"I have no intention of breaking her heart."

"I don't think you would do it intentionally. Just, please be careful. Careful what you say and what you do. Don't lead her on." She turned and walked back to the kitchen before Sarah had a chance to respond.

Sarah set the table feeling a little off balance by the conversation. She didn't feel attacked. More like scolded. Warned. Her feelings for Lindsey were real. She wasn't leading her on. Her intentions were honorable. It was obvious how much Cricket cared for Lindsey. Sarah couldn't blame her for trying to protect her. She was determined to prove to Cricket and to Lindsey that she meant what she said.

"How ya doing?" She hadn't heard Lindsey come up behind her.

"Okay."

"Sarah, did Cricket say something to you?"

Her first thought was to brush it off. She didn't want to come between Lindsey and her friend. But lying to Lindsey was something she never wanted to do. "It was nothing. She was just being protective."

"I could tell by the look on your face that something was up. I'm going to talk to her."

"No, don't. Please," Sarah said. "She wasn't mean or anything. She cares about you. I think she just wanted to make sure I did too. And I do, you know. Care about you. A lot."

Lindsey believed her. She wished she had thought to tell Cricket not to get on Sarah's case. She knew Cricket did it out of love, but it really wasn't her place to say anything.

"Don't be mad at her," Sarah said. "She was being a good friend. Looking out for you."

"I'm a big girl. I don't need anyone looking out for me."

"Hey. We can all use someone in our corner sometimes," Sarah said. "Please don't say anything to her. Besides, she'll think I tattled on her."

Lindsey smiled. "You don't want her to know you're a snitch? A rat?"

"Hey, you're the one who asked."

"Are we going to eat or what?" Cricket called from the kitchen.

Lindsey shook her head. "That's Cricket. You're going to love her—eventually."

"I'm sure I will. I just hope she likes me."

Lindsey put her arm around Sarah's shoulder. Sarah knew it was just a gesture of friendship, but it was a good sign. "She is going to love you too."

"Sure. What's not to love?"

"I love how modest you are. Did I ever mention that?" Lindsey asked.

"I don't believe you have. But feel free to mention it often."

"You got it. Now let's get the food on the table before Cricket eats her own arm off. Or worse yet—mine."

Lindsey watched the interaction between Sarah and Cricket with interest during dinner. Whatever Cricket had said to Sarah didn't seem to be a barrier. They chatted with ease.

"I've never seen that movie," Sarah said.

"I highly recommend it. The writing is excellent. It's hard to find a movie with such a great message, that they sneak in instead of shoving it down your throat," Cricket said.

"I'll have to check it out." Sarah turned her attention to Lindsey. "Have you seen it?"

"I have, but it's good enough to watch again, if you want company when you watch it."

"I would love that," Sarah said. Her wide smile made Lindsey smile in return. "How about tomorrow evening?"

"Or we could watch it here after I kick Cricket out."

"Hey!" Cricket said.

"Trevor, you can stay if you want," Lindsey added.

"Trevor goes where I go. Isn't that right, honey?"

"Of course," Trevor said. "I would follow you to the ends of the earth." He lowered his voice and put his hand to the side of his mouth. "Was that the right answer?"

"Perfect. Just like you," Cricket responded.

"I'm going to get diabetes from listening to you two," Lindsey said.

"You're just jealous," Cricket said. "It will happen for you too."

Lindsey snuck a glance at Sarah. She was sipping her wine and Lindsey wasn't sure if she had paid attention to their exchange or not. She hoped she hadn't. Or maybe she hoped she had. It was all so confusing.

"So, what do you think, Sarah? About staying to watch the movie?" Lindsey asked.

"Sure. That sounds great."

"You can stay too, Cricket," Lindsey said, knowing she wouldn't.

"Thanks for the invite, but we're going to go after we finish eating. You know me. I'm an eat-and-run kind of gal."

Lindsey silently mouthed the words *thank you.*

True to her word, Cricket and Trevor left shortly after everyone finished their food. She did, however, offer to help clean up, but Lindsey insisted she had it covered. As much as she loved her friend she was looking forward to some alone time with Sarah.

Lindsey put the leftovers in the fridge and Sarah helped her put the dishes in the dishwasher.

"Would you like me to wash that?" Sarah pointed to a pot on the stove.

"Nope, I'll do it in the morning. Let's relax in the living room and watch that movie. Would you like me to open another bottle of wine?"

Sarah seemed to think about it for a few moments. "Sure, why not?"

"Make yourself comfortable on the couch and I'll be there in a minute." Lindsey retrieved a bottle, opened it, and grabbed two clean glasses. Sarah was sitting a little left of center on the couch when Lindsey made her way to the living room. She set the glasses on the coffee table and poured the wine. She handed one to Sarah as she tried to decide where to sit—in the chair, away from Sarah, or on the couch next to her. If she chose the couch, they would only be inches apart. The fact that she *wanted* to sit next to Sarah was the exact reason that she thought she shouldn't.

"Do you want some popcorn?" Lindsey asked, trying to buy more time to decide.

"Oh no. I'm still full from dinner. But you go ahead if you want."

Oh, what the hell. We're both grownups. Nothing is going to happen. She sat next to her. They were close enough that Lindsey could feel the heat coming off Sarah's body. Or was that her own body heating up for being so close?

"Did you have a nice time?" Lindsey picked up her wine glass and took a sip.

"Yes. It's been a very pleasant evening. Thank you. I can see why Cricket is your best friend. She seems like a lot of fun."

"Yeah, when she isn't harassing my—" She almost said girlfriend but stopped herself. "My other friend."

"She was just being protective. I don't blame her. I would have felt the same way she did."

"I still don't—"

"Stop," Sarah interrupted. "It's fine. Honest. Should we start the movie?"

Lindsey found the remote on the end table, did a quick search, and started the show. She reached over and turned off the lamp on the end table. *Much better.*

They were halfway thought the movie when Lindsey realized that Sarah was leaning against her shoulder and her head was tilted at an odd angle to the side. Sarah's rhythmic breathing told Lindsey she had fallen asleep. Lindsey wasn't sure whether to wake her or not. She lowered the volume on the TV and whispered Sarah's name. She didn't respond.

Lindsey eased herself away from Sarah, holding onto her shoulder so she didn't flop over and lowered her down to the couch. Sarah didn't wake up. Lindsey went to her bedroom closet, pulled down a blanket from the shelf, and grabbed a pillow off her bed.

She gently lifted Sarah's head, put a pillow under it, lowered her back down, and covered her with the blanket. She turned the TV off and went into the kitchen to finish cleaning up. Sarah was still asleep when she finished. Various possibilities and scenarios went through her mind. She could go to bed and leave Sarah sleeping on the couch or she could wake her up. If she left her sleeping, Sarah would probably be disoriented when she did wake up. If she woke her up, she might insist on driving home and would probably still be groggy. She decided on her third choice, wake her up, give her something to wear and let her spend the night.

Lindsey got a T-shirt and a pair of sweatpants from her bedroom, set them on a chair in the living room and turned on the lamp. "Sarah," she whispered, gently shaking her shoulder. She repeated her name a little louder.

"Huh." Sarah opened her eyes and blinked a few times. She sat up. "Oh, wow. Did I fall asleep? I'm so sorry. I should go."

"No. No. I don't think you should drive. Why don't you spend the night?"

Sarah looked at her and Lindsey could see the question in her eyes.

"You can take my bed and I'll sleep on the couch. I got you something to wear," Lindsey said.

"I can't take your bed. I didn't drink that much. I'll be okay to drive."

Lindsey still was unconvinced. If anything happened to Sarah on her way home, Lindsey would never forgive herself. "You must be really tired. I would feel better if you spent the night. If it would make you more comfortable, you can sleep on the couch. I've got clothes that you can wear to work tomorrow if you don't want to stop home to change."

"I don't want to be an imposition."

"You aren't. I want you to stay." And she did. It was a comforting thought to have Sarah in her house. Close by.

"Are you sure?"

"I'm positive. Why don't you change in the bathroom. There's a new toothbrush in the top drawer on the right-hand side of the sink. Toothpaste is in the medicine cabinet."

Sarah yawned. "Okay. You're probably right."

"I usually am," Lindsey said with a laugh.

"Good to know. I'll keep that in mind." Sarah stood, and Lindsey handed her the night clothes she'd grabbed. "Thank you. What are you doing tomorrow evening?"

"Well, it is Friday, and most people have big plans then. But me—nothing. Why?"

"I'm having my art show opening. It would be great if you could come, if you're still interested."

Lindsey had forgotten all about that even though she had it on her calendar. "Yes. Yes. I would love to go."

Sarah laughed. "Then it's a date. Sorry. Didn't mean that. It's two friends going to one friend's art opening." She pointed at herself. "This is me respecting your wishes and your boundaries."

Lindsey almost regretted putting those boundaries in place. Almost. She still needed to keep that shield around her heart. At least for a little while longer. She needed to be sure that Sarah meant what she said and wouldn't go running off—or push Lindsey away—out of fear again. "Go ahead and get ready for bed—or the couch. Your choice."

"The couch. But thank you for the offer of your bed. I just wouldn't feel right."

"Okay. I want you to be comfortable."

"I'm sure the couch will be fine. It was comfortable enough to fall asleep on. Sorry about that. I missed most of the movie."

"No problem. We'll catch it another time." She watched as she padded off to the bathroom. It only took a few minutes for her to return. She looked damn cute in Lindsey's clothes. "What else do you need?" she asked.

Sarah set her neatly folded clothes on the chair. "I'm all set. I really appreciate this."

"Of course." Lindsey got a glass of water from the kitchen and set it on the coffee table. "Have a good night. I'll see you in the morning." Lindsey couldn't help but look forward to waking up and having Sarah there.

"Good night."

Lindsey locked the doors and shut off all the lights except for the lamp on the end table. After getting herself ready for bed, she slipped under the covers. It had been a good evening. She enjoyed meeting and getting to know Trevor and she always liked having Cricket around. But having Sarah in the mix made it extra special.

As tired as she was, sleep was a long time coming. Sarah was just in the other room. She so wanted to go in there and... *No. Don't let your brain go there.* So close, yet so far. It was well after one o'clock in the morning by the time she fell asleep.

Sarah was still asleep when Lindsey tiptoed past her to make coffee the next morning. She usually only made enough for a single cup, which was her limit, but set it to make a full pot. She had no idea how much coffee Sarah drank—or if she even drank it at all.

Sarah was sitting up when she passed though the living room again. "Good morning. How'd you sleep?"

"Good. Your couch is very comfortable."

"I'm glad. Do you want to come and pick out some clothes for today?"

"I think I'll stop home and change. I don't have to be to work till nine."

"I just put a pot of coffee on. Do you drink coffee?"

"Yes. Thank you. I'm going to go get dressed."

Lindsey sat on the arm of the couch. "Of course. Can I make you something for breakfast? Eggs? Pancakes? Toast?"

"Wow. The service around here is great. I should stay at this place more often. I'm definitely giving it four and a half stars on Yelp." She grabbed her pile of clothes from the chair.

"Only four and a half? Why not five stars?"

"It gives you incentive to improve. Not that I'm saying you need improvement."

"That's exactly what it sounds like to me. You weren't completely satisfied." *I'll satisfy you. Oh my God. Stop it, brain.*

"It gives you something to work toward." Sarah laughed. "Do you normally eat breakfast?"

"It's kind of hit or miss. If I don't *hit* the snooze button too often, I get up early enough to eat. If I do, then I'm usually running late so I *miss* it."

"Oh. I see what you did there. Very clever. If you have time for breakfast, then yes. Any of the above would be great. I don't want you to go to too much trouble."

You're going to be trouble. Good trouble. Her brain was working overtime with quick comebacks that she didn't dare say. "No trouble. Get dressed. I'll get breakfast ready."

Sarah gave her a quick salute and was off to the bathroom with her clothes. She returned to the scent of bacon wafting through the air. "That smells great." The last thing she expected when Lindsey invited her to dinner was to fall asleep during a movie and end up spending the night. She had to admit to herself that waking up and seeing Lindsey's face first thing in the morning was nice—even if it wasn't from across the bed. And Lindsey agreed to accompany her to the art show. She seemed to even be excited about it. Life was looking up. Maybe she hadn't blown it after all.

"Thank you for everything," Sarah said as they finished breakfast. "I hate to eat and run, but I'm going to have to eat and run."

"Oh sure. Eat and run," Lindsey said. "And you're welcome." She walked Sarah to the door and gave her a hug. "See you on Friday. I'm sure we'll talk before then."

Sarah held the hug several seconds longer than your average friendship hug—if there was such a thing. She didn't want to let go. She held Lindsey's gaze when she finally pulled back. She was pretty sure she saw hope there. That's what she felt as well. Hope. It was a long time coming. She didn't think it was possible even a few weeks ago. "Bye," she whispered.

"Bye." Lindsey kept the door open, watching as Sarah got into her car and drove away. She was still standing there when Sarah turned the corner, and she could no longer see Lindsey's house in her rearview mirror. But she could feel her in her heart. A heart that opened up to the possibilities that life had to offer.

CHAPTER SEVENTEEN

"I'm so nervous," Sarah said to Lindsey. "I've never liked being the center of attention."

"You've got this. I'll be right there by your side, supporting you the whole way. Your art is incredible. If it helps, think of that as the center of attention."

Sarah was so thankful to have Lindsey with her at the gallery. And she'd been kind enough to drive. That helped a lot. They'd come in the back door and were sitting on a couch in the gallery office.

"How are you doing?" Diane, the gallery owner, asked her.

"Nervous."

"Oh stop. You've done this before. You're always a pro. I have no doubts this will go well."

But this was the first time she'd done it without Julie. Julie had been her rock.

Lindsey took her hand and smiled at her. "I have full faith you can handle this. I'm here." Sarah smiled back. She still had a rock. A new rock. She was open to that and grateful. "Thank you."

"Deep breath," Diane said. "We are starting to get people milling about outside, waiting to come in. I'm going to open the doors. Are you ready?"

"Ready as I'll ever be."

"Shall we?" Lindsey asked, waving toward the door that led to the gallery. "I can't wait to see your work."

Sarah nodded and followed Lindsey into the gallery area. There were already several people milling about. Lindsey had only seen the first painting that Sarah had done for this show, so she followed as Lindsey wandered around.

"You should be so proud of yourself," Lindsey said. "These are so beautiful. Am I allowed to buy one?"

"Which one did you like?" Sarah asked.

"This one." They were standing in front of a sixteen-by-twenty framed painting of a garden, filled with flowers and with a small cottage and several trees in the background. She'd taken the reference picture on a trip to Italy almost ten years earlier. The picture had been on her computer all that time, waiting to be re-created as art.

"Why this one?" Sarah asked.

"This tree in the background. It's a fig tree. It looks just like the one in my grandmother's yard." Lindsey felt connected to it the minute she saw it. All the paintings were beautiful. This one was special.

"Excuse me." A woman had come up behind them. "Are you the artist?"

Sarah turned to her. "I am."

"Your work is exquisite." She handed Sarah her business card. "I own a gallery in New York City. I would love to have you featured in a show we are planning for December. Is there somewhere we can talk for a few minutes?"

"Of course," Sarah said. She looked at Lindsey.

"Yes. Go ahead, I'm going to finish looking around." She watched as Sarah led the woman into the gallery office. She was excited for the possibility of another show for Sarah, especially in a big city like New York.

She wandered around taking in the other paintings and listening to conversations of others looking at the art. There were so many positive comments. Lindsey felt proud for Sarah. Her art was being so well received.

Diane came around the corner and placed a small red dot sticker on the title card under the painting of the Italian garden that Lindsey had liked so much. "What's that for?" Lindsey asked.

"It means it's sold." Diane continued to another painting at the end of the display and placed another dot. Lindsey's heart sank. She should have purchased the painting as soon as she saw it. She wondered if Sarah would be willing to paint something similar, with a fig tree in it or if she should even ask.

"That was an interesting meeting," Sarah said as she rejoined Lindsey. "Diane said we've already sold a couple of pieces."

"That's great," Lindsey said, trying to hide her disappointment. "How did it go with that lady from New York?"

"Good. I think there's a real possibility to have a show there. It sounds like she has a good size gallery."

"Wonderful. Everyone seems to be loving your work. I've taken it upon myself to eavesdrop as much as possible."

"I didn't know you were good at that."

"I am. Almost a pro, if I do say so myself, and obviously—I do."

Sarah laughed. "I'm so glad you're here with me."

"Me too. Thanks for inviting me."

Diane came up to them with a couple in tow. "And this is the artist, Sarah Osborn," she said to them. "Sarah, this is Mr. and Mrs. O'Neal. They just bought the painting on the end, *Sunkissed Bouquet*."

"So nice to meet you," Sarah said.

"I fell in love with that piece the moment I laid eyes on it," Mrs. O'Neal squealed. "It reminds me so much of my own flowers. You are so talented."

Lindsey took a tiny step back, letting Sarah enjoy the praise lavished upon her and her work. She didn't know why Sarah had been so nervous. She was so good with people.

Two more paintings sold by the end of the evening and the show would be up till the end of the month, so it was likely that even more would sell. "I'm so proud of you," Lindsey said on the drive back to Sarah's. "You did great, not only creating your art, but the way you handled yourself all evening. You were so kind and attentive with everyone that you talked to."

"Thank you," Sarah said. "I fake it well. I feel so out of my element. I mean, creating the art is so solitary, being in public with it is certainly stepping out of my comfort zone."

"You do it so well. No one could tell you were nervous. I certainly couldn't. And you sold four paintings. That's amazing."

"Three," Sarah said.

"I thought it was four."

"Nope. Just three."

"Well, that is still great." Lindsey pulled into Sarah's driveway.

"Would you like to come in?" Sarah asked.

Lindsey wanted to. Way too much. "I better not," she said. "It's late. It was a great day. Thanks for including me."

"Anytime."

"Six o'clock tomorrow," Lindsey said.

"Huh?"

"You said anytime. So how about six o'clock tomorrow? I would like to take you out—on a date," Lindsey said, surprising herself. "I mean if you're still interested in that. In this. In us. I mean in the possibilities." Why was she stumbling over her words. It wasn't like they didn't already know and like each other.

Sarah tilted her head and looked at her. Lindsey thought maybe she was trying to figure out if she was serious or not.

"Yes. I said it. If you're interested, I would like to take you out on an actual date." Was it Lindsey's imagination or did Sarah sit up a little straighter? And the smile that spread across her face was a good sign.

"I would be very interested. Yes."

She hadn't planned on formally asking Sarah out, but it seemed like the thing to do in the moment. She knew she liked her. She understood her reasoning for her reaction after they'd had sex. She was starting to trust her again. There was nothing holding them back. Cricket's words about not getting caught up in her feelings echoed in the back of her mind, but she ignored them. This was the right thing to do. She knew it with every fiber of her being. It was the right step, at the right time. At least for her. She believed it was for Sarah too. And if that smile that hadn't faded one bit, was any indication, it was.

"Yes?" Lindsey repeated. "Great. Pick you up about six? Dinner, maybe a movie?"

"I would like that. Very much."

Lindsey leaned across the seat and kissed Sarah on the cheek. As much as she wanted to kiss her full on the mouth she didn't. Not yet anyway. They needed to take this slow. Well, as slow as she was able to. It wasn't going to be easy. But she knew it would be worth it.

❖

Sarah changed her clothes three times. Why was she so nervous? It was just a date. Their first official date. She was being ridiculous. She finally settled on gray dress slacks, a light blue button-down shirt with vertical pleats down the front, and black flats. She slipped a gold chain, with a garnet, around her neck. It had been a gift from Julie for their second anniversary. It felt good to bring a little bit of Julie with her. She didn't think Lindsey would mind. Not that she planned on telling her.

How much things can change in a few weeks, Sarah thought. Hell, even a day could make a difference. Yesterday, she was hoping she and Lindsey could make their way back to friendship. And now she could look forward to an actual date with her. She checked in with her heart—to the part that stored her love for Julie. To her surprise there was no guilt. "Thank you for teaching me how to love, Julie," she said into the air. "And thank you for allowing me to move on." She was looking forward to exactly that. Moving on.

Lindsey arrived right on time. Sarah checked herself in the mirror before answering the door.

Lindsey looked beautiful in her moderately low-cut maroon, shimmering shirt that showed just a peek of cleavage, and black pants. The small amount of makeup enhanced her already beautiful features.

"You look nice," Lindsey said.

"Ditto. Come on in. I'm almost ready." She stepped back to let Lindsey pass.

"Be right back. Go ahead and have a seat." Sarah went into the bathroom, ran a brush through her hair one more time, and gave it spritz of hairspray. She dabbed a touch of perfume behind each ear. She wasn't a big fan of over-smelling, as Julie called it.

"Ready," she said as she entered the living room.

"Excellent."

Sarah followed Lindsey outside. Lindsey opened the car door for her and then went around to the driver's side.

"I'm glad we're doing this," Sarah said.

"Me too."

The restaurant was crowded, but they were seated right away when Lindsey mentioned they had reservations.

They made small talk after they placed their drink orders. "What are you thinking of getting?" Lindsey asked as they perused the menu.

"It all looks so good. I have no idea. You?" Sarah tended to order from the middle range of prices when out with someone else. She didn't want to appear cheap or over extravagant.

"I have no idea what to get either."

They'd made up their minds by the time the waitress returned with their drinks and took their orders. It didn't take long for their meals to arrive. "How's your chicken?" Lindsey asked.

"Excellent. Want to try it?"

"Sure."

Sarah cut a piece and offered it across the table on her fork. She watched Lindsey's mouth as open and accept it. Her mind went back to them on the couch and what that mouth had done to her. The memory made her wet. If only she hadn't been such an ass afterward. Where would they be now? A first date was a great step, but they could have been so much further along. There could have been many nights—mornings and afternoons—of lovemaking. She squirmed in her seat against the reaction of her body at the thought.

"You okay?" Lindsey asked.

Sarah had hoped Lindsey hadn't noticed, but apparently, she did. "Fine. Do you like the chicken?"

"Yes. It's very good." Lindsey cut a piece of her steak and offered it across the table. Sarah allowed Lindsey to put it in her mouth. She chewed slowly, enjoying it. "That's good, too."

"Want more?" Lindsey asked.

Sarah shook her head. "I'm good."

"I know you are," Lindsey said with a wink.

Sarah hoped that the heat working its way up from her neck to her face wasn't turning her skin beet red. Her libido seemed to be in full swing. "How was work?" she asked, trying to take her attention off sex.

"It was okay. Nothing special."

"Do you like what you do?"

Lindsey scrounged up her face. "I like my coworkers. Cricket has the cubicle next to mine and she rarely stays in it. She's in mine so often that I worry she's going to get fired. But she gets her work done. Somehow. So, I guess she's good. The job itself is kind of boring. It pays the bills."

"If you could do anything in the world for a living, what would you do?"

"I'm not sure. Being a movie star seems like it would be fun."

Sarah laughed. "The money would probably be good, but I would think the fame would be a pain in the ass."

"You're probably right. I'll scratch that one off my list." She sipped her drink. "I'd love to run a nursery."

"Like with babies?" Sarah asked.

Lindsey laughed and Sarah made a note to try to make her laugh more often. It made her even more beautiful, pulling Sarah in. "No," Lindsey said. "Like plants. I am fascinated watching the fig cuttings root and grow. I mean, you take these things that look like sticks, and you can get them to grow into trees. The miracle of nature is amazing. I just love it. All plants really. I love growing them."

"You should do more of that. You light up when you talk about it."

"I'd like to. I was going to plant a garden, but the time kind of got away from me. Next year for sure."

"Julie was the gardener in our family. Roses were her specialty."

"How come I didn't see any roses around your house?" Lindsey took a bite of her food.

"They're in the back yard along the fence. I'm afraid they've been very neglected since she died."

"I can help with that." Lindsey paused. "I mean, if you want. I don't know how you would feel about me touching Julie's roses."

Sarah wiped a bit of something off the corner of her mouth. "Don't be silly. I would love it if you could help me with them. They probably need to be trimmed or fertilized or something."

"I'll come tomorrow and take a look, if you're going to be home."

If Lindsey was coming over, Sarah would be sure she was home. "That would be great. I would really appreciate it. I've felt bad that I've let them go so long."

"Would you quit your job and do art full-time if you could?" Lindsey asked.

Sarah had to think about it. She tilted her head. "Hmm. No. I don't think so. I enjoy my job. It's kind of the opposite of art. Art is creative. My job is more analytical. Between the art and my work, I get to use both sides of my brain. I like that. Besides, making a living doing art is nearly impossible."

"But you're so good at it." Lindsey finished the last bite of her food and moved her plate off to the side. "I mean your art show was amazing. You sold pieces the first night."

"Thank you. It's not that I don't like it. But I like my job too. Speaking of the art show..." She paused long enough to pull something from her pocket. She handed the folded piece of paper to Lindsey. "I wanted you to have this."

"What is it?" Lindsey asked.

"Open it and find out." She was excited to see her reaction.

Lindsey unfolded it and looked at the photo of the painting with the fig tree that she'd liked from Sarah's show. She looked confused. "Is this a print of the painting I liked?"

"Why yes. Yes, it is. But..." she let the word drift off. "I wouldn't give you a print on a folded-up piece of paper. "I had Diane mark it as sold because I want to give it to you. The original painting, I mean." She smiled and expected Lindsey to do the same. She didn't.

"I can't take that. I wanted to buy it, not have you give it to me. You've got way too much time and work into it to be giving it away."

"I'm not giving it to just anyone. I'm giving it to you. You've opened up my world again. It's my way of saying thank you. And if it brings a little of your grandmother back to you, well, that would be a bonus."

"At least let me pay you for it," Lindsey said.

"Fair enough. It's five dollars. Cash, Venmo, or PayPal. No checks. Oh, and there is a one-dollar delivery fee. Of course, you can always pick it up at my house after the show closes. It needs to stay up until then."

There it was. The smile Sarah had been hoping to see. "I don't know what to say," Lindsey said.

"I believe thank you, Sarah, you're the best, would be appropriate," Sarah said with a smile.

"Thank you, Sarah. You're the best. Painting or no painting. You're the best. I'll Venmo you the money tonight."

"Good. That money will come in very handy. I need to buy a new pair of shoes."

"I don't think five dollars is going to get you what you need," Lindsey said.

"You didn't let me finish. Shoe—laces. I need shoelaces."

"Oh, in that case you should be all set." There was that smile again.

The waitress returned, refilled their water glasses, and cleared their plates. "Did you leave room for dessert? The strawberry cheesecake is delicious."

"None for me," Sarah said. "Lindsey?"

"I'm all set. Thanks. Just the check please."

"Of course," the waitress said. "Be right back with it."

They had a brief discussion over who was going to pay the bill with Lindsey declared the winner, with the privilege of paying the tip going to Sarah. She was glad she'd thought to pocket some cash before leaving the house.

The ride back to Sarah's house was quick. Too quick. Sarah didn't want to see the evening end. Lindsey walked her to the door. "Would you like to come in?" Sarah asked.

"Probably not the best idea," Lindsey said with a smile.

There was a moment where it seemed like they were both trying to decide what was an appropriate ending to their date. Sarah wanted to kiss Lindsey but thought it was best to let Lindsey lead the way. Lindsey pulled her in for a hug and kissed her on the cheek. *Okay, better than nothing.* Lindsey gave her an extra squeeze before releasing her. They stood on the stoop several more seconds with their eyes locked on one another. Lindsey leaned in for a split second and Sarah was sure she was going to kiss her. But Lindsey pulled back. Disappointment seeped in around the edges and Sarah did her best not to let it show. She was surprised when Lindsey pulled her in for another hug.

"I had a really nice time," Lindsey said close to Sarah's ear, sending shivers down Sarah's back.

"Me too."

Lindsey pulled back just enough to look into Sarah's eyes before diving in with both lips, planting a kiss on Sarah's mouth, which Sarah opened, inviting Lindsey's tongue in.

The silent invitation was accepted, and Lindsey explored Sarah mouth, pulling their bodies closer together. Lindsey felt Sarah tremble. She ended the kiss as quickly as she had started it. Any longer and she was sure they would end up in Sarah's bed, and she didn't want that. Well, she did. A lot. But she knew it was a bad idea. They needed to go slowly. *She* needed to go slowly.

"Umm. Okay. I should get going," Lindsey said, struggling to get the words out. The kiss had left her breathless. Apparently, that wasn't something that only happened in books.

Sarah nodded, seemingly with the same problem.

Lindsey released her and slid her hands into her pocket to avoid the temptation of pulling Sarah back in for more.

"Text me when you get home?" Sarah said. "I want to make sure you're safe."

That touched Lindsey's heart. No one except her grandmother had ever wanted her to check in to make sure she was okay. "I will. Thank you for a great evening."

"Ditto. Talk to you tomorrow."

Lindsey waited until Sarah unlocked the door and went inside before she walked back to her car. It had been a great evening indeed. She thought she'd connected with Tina, but that paled in comparison to what she felt when she was with Sarah. Her mind went back to something her grandmother had told her when she was young, and she didn't get something she wanted. "Sometimes blessings come when God says no." She hadn't really thought about the true meaning of that until now. If Tina hadn't walked out, she never would have met Sarah. She only answered her email because she thought they had something in common. Funny how things worked out.

She started her car and sent up a silent prayer of thanks to her grandmother. She knew this was only a first step with Sarah, but she was so looking forward to the next step and the hundreds after that.

❖

Lindsey stopped at the garden store—the one near Sarah's house, not the one that Ginny worked at. She didn't need that headache again. She picked up pruning shears, heavy-duty gardening gloves and rose fertilizer, then headed to Sarah's and rang the doorbell. She was greeted with an ear-to-ear grin. The jeans she had on were ripped in the knees and the T-shirt had paint stains on it. "Hi there." She looked beautiful.

"Hi. I've come ready to work." Lindsey held up her equipment. "Take me to your roses. Get it? Like take me to your leader but with roses." She laughed at her own silliness. "Never mind. Ignore me."

Sarah turned her head and yelled into the house. "Honey, the gardener's here."

"Does the gardener get a kiss?" Lindsey asked.

Sarah turned her head again and yelled. "Honey, the gardener wants to know if she can have a kiss?"

Lindsey waited a few moments. "What was the answer?"

"No. I'm only supposed to kiss the pool boy."

"Do you even have a pool?"

"Good point. No pool. I guess I can kiss the gardener." She took a step forward and kissed Lindsey on the cheek.

"That was lame."

"Too bad you aren't the pool boy. You should see the kiss he gets."

Lindsey turned around and headed back toward her car.

"Hey. Where are you going?" Sarah called after her.

Lindsey turned. "I'm going to get stuff to clean your nonexistent pool. I want a better kiss."

"Get over here, you crazy woman. I'll kiss you."

Lindsey rushed back. "Okay. That was easy."

"Are you saying I'm easy?" Sarah asked.

"You," Lindsey said, "are anything but easy."

"Now you're saying I'm difficult? You're digging yourself quite the hole."

"I didn't say that. Let me rephrase. You are perfect in every way."

"That's better. Come on in. I'll kiss the hell out of you."

Lindsey stepped inside and Sarah closed the door behind them. She wrapped her arms around Lindsey and kissed her. Hard. Passionately.

Lindsey's body was on fire by the time Sarah let her up for air. "Wow. I can only imagine how much better that would have been if I was a pool boy."

Sarah pulled her in for another kiss, sending Lindsey's head spinning.

Lindsey reluctantly pulled out of it. "If we don't stop your roses aren't going to get—"

Sarah kissed her again and Lindsey was immediately wet, and she tightened her muscles against it. It only made the feeling more intense. She was tempted to walk Sarah to the bedroom and make love with her. She pulled out of the kiss and blew out a puff of air to try to ground herself.

"Too much?" Sarah asked.

"Just enough. Believe me, that's all I can take at the moment." Anymore and she wouldn't be in control. Her body would be.

"What else did you want to do if you can't take any more kissing?"

"Roses," Lindsey said. "Roses."

"Would you like anything to eat or drink first?" Sarah released her tight grip on Lindsey.

Lindsey had eaten breakfast before stopping at the garden store. "No, thanks. Did you eat?"

"I did. We can go outside if you're ready."

"Okay," Lindsey said. "Lead the way." She followed Sarah out the back door and onto the deck.

The yard was surprisingly big. It was a little wider than the width of the house, but it went quite a ways back. The whole thing was surrounded by a white picket fence, more for aesthetics than for privacy. Two badly neglected flower beds edged the deck. Several out-of-control rose bushes pushed up against the back fence. An old wooden shed stood off to the side.

"I know," Sarah said. "It's terrible. I feel bad."

"Nothing that can't be fixed. What would you think if we go to the store after I take care of the roses and get some flowers for me to plant?"

"I would love that," Sarah said. "Are you sure you want to do that? It seems like an awful lot of work."

"It's no trouble. I'm going to have you help me pull weeds though. We can get some knee pads to make it easier on you."

"I'm sure there must be some in the shed. That's were Julie had all her tools."

"Great. I'll get started, and you can get whatever you think we'll need for that."

Lindsey set to work trimming the dead wood off the roses and thinning them out. She pulled as many of the weeds between the plants that she could without the thorns tearing up her arms. She was pleased when she finished and stepped back to admire her work.

"That looks wonderful." Sarah had been watching her from a chair on the deck. There was a box of tools she dug out of the shed at her feet and a pitcher of lemonade and two glasses on the table next to her. She felt bad that Lindsey was doing all the work, but she had no idea how to help. Lindsey really seemed to know what she was doing.

"Thanks," Lindsey said.

"Take a break and have something to drink."

Lindsey sat and pulled off her gloves. Several small beads of sweat peppered her forehead. It made her look sexier, if that was even possible.

Sarah poured the lemonade and handed a glass to Lindsey. They made quick work of it and headed to the store. Forty minutes later, they were back with two trays of various flowers, a couple of bags of mulch, and a bag of food from Burger King.

After a quick lunch, they set to work pulling weeds and planting the flowers. They stood back to admire their work. "This will look even better once we put the mulch down," Lindsey said.

Sarah agreed. She loved having Lindsey around, with them working side by side. She was, however, finding it hard to keep her hands off her. She wanted to touch her, to kiss her, to…well, everything. But she wanted to do it right this time. No rush. No fumbling around on the couch. No asking Lindsey to leave afterward. She would regret that move for the rest of her life.

She wanted to sleep with her head on Lindsey's shoulder. Wake up with Lindsey next to her. Feel the weight of Lindsey's body on top of hers. She wanted Lindsey. That about summed it up.

"What are you thinking about?"

"You." Sarah said.

"What about me?"

"How much I want you. In every way possible. Maybe every position possible." No sense beating around the bush. She wanted Lindsey and wasn't afraid to say it. She watched Lindsey to try to gauge her reaction. She saw her swallow. Hard. Was that a good sign or a bad sign? "Say something."

"Every position possible?"

Sarah felt the heat rising up from her chest. "Yes."

"Umm. Okay."

"Okay? What does that mean?"

"I mean I've never had anyone tell me that before."

Sarah wasn't sure whether to push for a real answer or not. She decided it was better not to. If it was something Lindsey wanted as well, she would have to be the one to make the first move. Sarah had voiced it. That was as far as she was going.

Lindsey's heart kicked up a beat or two. Yes, she wanted Sarah. But to act on it wasn't taking things slowly. How dangerous would it be if she gave Sarah her body so soon? She knew where her body went her heart would follow. Oh, who was she kidding? Sarah already had her heart. She had it soon after they met. Lindsey's questions weren't about her feelings and intentions. They were about Sarah's.

Sarah seemed sincere, but could she be trusted not to flip-flop again and pull back? Lindsey knew that if that happened again it would be the end. The end of a potential relationship and the end of their friendship.

Questions. Questions. Questions. She couldn't be certain of the answers. She couldn't be certain of anything. Then again, she was certain about Tina and *her* feelings and look where that got her. Maybe the answer was there was no answer. It was impossible to know anything for certain. Love was a gamble. All she could do was jump in with both feet and hope that the ground underneath her didn't give way.

She looked at Sarah. She was probably waiting for some sort of response from Lindsey that wasn't so vague. She would have to wait a little longer. Lindsey dragged one of the bags of mulch closer to the flower garden and ripped it open. The silence between them was deafening. She reached into the bag and spread a handful of mulch carefully around the new plants. She reached in again and her hand touched Sarah's as she also attempted to grab a handful of mulch. The contact sent a tingle though Lindsey, landing squarely in her center. "Okay," she said. She laced her fingers though Sarah's. "Okay. You can have me. In every way. In every position." There was no sense fighting it anymore. They were both consenting adults and obviously were attracted to each other.

"What?"

"I want you too. So…" She let Sarah fill in the rest of her thought.

Sarah smiled. "Should we finish the mulch or just rip each other's clothes off right here?"

Sarah's words sent a hot chill through Lindsey. She looked around and laughed. "I'm sure your neighbors would appreciate the show, but I think we should finish the garden."

"Okay. We can do that. But I think the other idea might raise my stature in my neighbors' eyes. I can see it now. I'd be walking down the sidewalk and total strangers would high-five me."

"Oh, now you've got me feeling guilty for not helping you with that."

"That's okay. I'll get over it. Eventually," Sarah said with a smirk.

"Oh good. Let's get this done so we can go in." Lindsey knelt and spread some of the mulch toward the back of the garden. It didn't take them long to get it finished.

"I think I need a shower," Sarah said as they walked into the house. "I'm all kinds of sweaty."

"Me too."

"Would you like to join me?" Sarah raised her eyebrows. "I mean you shouldn't be walking around all sweaty."

"You wouldn't mind?" Lindsey was already wet, and they hadn't even stepped under the water yet.

"I don't mind. Maybe I'll let you wash my back while we're in there."

"Okay. If you think that would be helpful."

"I do." Sarah poured two glasses of water and handed one to Lindsey. She drank it, put the glass on the counter and followed Sarah upstairs and into the bathroom.

Sarah turned the water on in the shower and turned to Lindsey. Without a word, she lifted the bottom edge of Lindsey's T-shirt and pulled it over her head. She ran her hands over Lindsey's breasts, over her bra, before reaching behind her and undoing the clasps. Lindsey's nipples stood at attention at the touch. She sucked in a breath. She slipped her arms out and let her bra fall to the floor.

"Beautiful," Sarah whispered. She undid the snap on Lindsey's pants, pulled down the zipper, and slowly yanked them down along with her underpants until they were around Lindsey's ankles. Lindsey stepped out of them and kicked them off to the side.

Sarah ran a single finger from Lindsey's belly button to her center and slipped it into the slickness. "You're wet," she said. "I like."

Lindsey sucked in a breath. "I like, too." She gave herself several seconds to enjoy the sensations before she removed Sarah's clothes in the same manner. She took in the sight before her. She wanted Sarah. And Sarah wanted her. Lindsey could see it in her eyes.

They stepped into the shower one after the other. The water flowed over Lindsey's body, warming her and she pulled Sarah closer to her. She could feel Sarah's breasts press into her own, and she pressed her mouth to Sarah's.

Sarah's arms came around her and she cupped Lindsey's ass, lessening the space between them until it was nonexistent. She deepened the kiss that Lindsey had started, sweeping her tongue across Lindsey's lips and entering her mouth. Lindsey welcomed it in.

Lindsey managed to reach the bar of soap on the shelf behind Sarah without breaking the kiss. She rubbed the bar between her hands, replaced the soap, and ran her sudsy hands up and down the silky skin on Sarah's back and down to her butt. She ran them up Sarah's sides before rinsing them off in the shower spray. She slipped her hand between Sarah's legs. Sarah's arms tightened around her, and Sarah's arousal became her own.

Lindsey broke the kiss and pushed Sarah gently against the shower wall. She worked her way down Sarah's body, stopping at her breasts and sucked in a nipple. The gasp Sarah let out spurned her on. She moved to the other nipple, running her tongue around its circumference before sucking it between her lips. She gave it her full attention listening to the sounds of pleasure coming from Sarah. The sounds increased as she continued down until she was on her knees.

The warm water cascaded down her back. She separated Sarah's folds and tentatively tasted her with her tongue. Sarah's hands were on the back of her head, fingers tangled in her hair as if Lindsey needed encouragement to keep her head where it was. She plunged her tongue into Sarah.

Sarah sucked in a large breath of air. She wasn't sure if the heat in her body was from the steam in the shower or what Lindsey's talented tongue was doing to her. She didn't know if she could remain standing as the promise of an orgasm rose in her. No words came out when she opened her mouth to voice it. As if she could read her mind, Lindsey placed a hand on her stomach as if holding her in place.

When Lindsey pushed first one finger and then two into her while her tongue teased her most sensitive spot, Sarah couldn't hold back any longer and she climaxed with a shudder. She sucked in several breaths, blowing them out hard as she slowly came down from the ride.

She pulled Lindsey up and wrapped her arms around her.

"I don't know if you noticed," Lindsey said, "but I washed your back like you wanted me to."

Sarah shook her head and then nodded. She couldn't quite form words yet.

"Does that mean you noticed, or you didn't?" Lindsey asked.

Sarah shook her head again. She rested her head against Lindsey's. It took a few minutes for her to recover from her orgasm.

"How you doing?" Lindsey asked when Sarah stood up straighter and pulled back enough to look into Lindsey's eyes.

"Wow. Yeah. Good. Wow."

"Good," Lindsey said with a wide smile. "I think the water's starting to cool down."

"For some strange reason I hadn't noticed." Sarah reached around to the faucet handle and turned it more toward hot. It didn't seem to make a difference. "Hmm. That's weird. Maybe we should get out if you're getting chilled."

"You'll keep me warm, won't you?" Lindsey pulled her in tighter.

"Ooorrr…" Sarah drew out the word. "We can dry ourselves off and make use of my bed."

Lindsey smiled. "I can deal with that."

Sarah turned off the water, they stepped out, and she handed Lindsey a towel. Instead of drying herself, Lindsey rubbed the towel up and down Sarah's body, letting her fingers trail behind, enjoying the feeling of Sarah's skin.

Sarah wrapped her arms around Lindsey's waist, pulled her in close, and kissed her lightly on the mouth.

"You're all wet again," Lindsey said.

"I'm wet alright." She took the towel from Lindsey and worked to finish drying them both. "Bed," she said when she finished.

"Lead the way."

Sarah pulled the quilt and blanket back on the bed, crooked her finger, and motioned for Lindsey to come closer. She took her by the shoulders, turned her, and eased her down until she was sitting on the bed. "Lie on your stomach toward the middle," Sarah whispered.

Lindsey did as she was told and watched as Sarah disappeared back into the bathroom.

She returned with a bottle, twisted off the top, and poured something into her hand. After setting the bottle down on the nightstand, she rubbed her hands together and sat on the edge of the bed.

The smell of vanilla filled the air. Sarah spread the warm oil across Lindsey's shoulders, massaging her muscles. It felt delicious. Soothing. Arousing. Sarah worked her way down Lindsey's back, working each section with expert hands.

Lindsey closed her eyes and sighed as her body relaxed under Sarah's touch.

Sarah skimmed over Lindsey's butt and gently pushed her legs apart. Lindsey knew she was already wet, from the back rub. Sarah teased, rubbing gently and slowly between Lindsey's legs. Lindsey ached to have those fingers inside her. She attempted to roll onto her back, but Sarah stopped her.

"Not yet." Sarah applied more pressure and Lindsey squirmed against her fingers. It was pure torture. Delicious, mind-blowing torture. The pressure in Lindsey increased to the edge of an orgasm.

"Roll over," Sarah said.

Lindsey complied. The throbbing between her legs wasn't subsiding and she sucked in a breath.

"Lindsey, open your eyes and look at me."

Lindsey blinked a few times before holding Sarah's gaze.

Sarah ran two fingers between Lindsey's folds and slipped them inside her. The rhythm of her movements seemed to match the rhythm of Lindsey's rapidly increasing heart rate. Sarah brought her to the edge and then backed off a bit, delaying Lindsey's orgasm.

Lindsey wanted to beg her for release, but the look and slight smile on Sarah's face told her not to. Sarah was in control, and she knew it.

Sarah continued moving her fingers at a pace that was enough to keep Lindsey aroused but not enough to put her over the edge. Without warning, Sarah pushed her fingers deep, leaned over, and ran her tongue over Lindsey, sucking on her swollen flesh.

Lindsey slammed her eyes shut as fireworks erupted through her body and her hips lifted from the bed, increasing the pressure from Sarah's tongue against her. She let out a loud moan.

The sounds coming from Lindsey as she climaxed sent new waves of arousal through Sarah and she was immediately wet all over again. She soaked up the power and pleasure of making Lindsey orgasm.

She slowly slipped her fingers out, but continued the pressure from her tongue, moving it in gentle circles. She felt Lindsey tugging at her. She lifted her head and turned to her. "Yes? Something you wanted?"

"Get up here," Lindsey said in a husky voice.

Sarah stretched out next to her and traced lazy circles around her still erect nipples. "How's it going?"

Lindsey blew out a breath. "Seems to be going good. You?"

"Excellent. Did you want to go finish the gardening now?"

"Umm. I think I need a few minutes, but you go ahead if you want to."

Sarah started to get up, but Lindsey pulled her back down. "What are you doing?"

"I was going to go put the tools back in the shed," Sarah said.

"Are you serious?"

Sarah snuggled in closer to Lindsey, wrapping her tightly in her arms. "Hell no. I'm not going anywhere." She looked into Lindsey's eyes and turned serious. "I mean it, Lindsey. I'm not going anywhere. I'm in this with both feet and my whole heart."

"Are you sure?" Lindsey asked.

Sarah nodded. Her eyes filled with tears, and it took her several seconds for her to be able to talk without crying. "I am absolutely sure. I'll do whatever it takes to prove it to you. She paused. "I know I screwed up in the past. But that's what it is—the past. It won't happen again. Ever." She brushed away the few tears that trailed down her cheek and smiled. "I mean I'm not perfect. Close. But not totally. I will mess up from time to time, but I love you and I'm promising you I'm going to do my best to make you happy."

"What?" Lindsey asked.

"I'll do my best to make you happy," Sarah repeated.

"No. No. Not that part. The part before that."

"The *I promise* part?"

"No. The love part. Do you really mean that or are you just caught up in the moment?" Lindsey asked. "Because I'm caught up in the moment, but I think I've loved you for quite a while now."

"You *think* you love me?"

"Wow," Lindsey said. "We seem to be having trouble just saying I love you. I'll fix that. I love you, Sarah Osborn. I truly, deeply love you."

"I love you too. This moment and the next and the ones after that. In fact, I'm planning on loving you forever."

EPILOGUE

L indsey gathered ingredients from the pantry along with eggs and milk from the refrigerator and set everything on the counter. Without measuring, she added each thing to a mixing bowl and stirred it until there were no more lumps. She sprayed the griddle on the stove with avocado oil and poured the batter into almost perfect circles.

"Hey, honey," Sarah said as she came into the kitchen. "Don't you think it's time to get ready?"

Lindsey put a cup of maple syrup in the microwave and set it for twenty seconds. "We have time. The wedding isn't till seven."

"Yeah, but you're the maid of honor. Don't you have to help Cricket get ready?"

"I talked to her a little while ago. Her mom is with her right now. I don't need to be there for quite a while." She flipped the pancakes over.

"Okay. Did she sound nervous?" Sarah asked.

"Not nearly as nervous as I was when we got married."

"You were only nervous because your mother was going to be there, and you weren't sure if she was going to behave herself."

"And it turned out I had nothing to worry about. She's come a long way." Lindsey plated up the pancakes, put a dab of butter on the top of each stack, and put them on the table. She grabbed the syrup and silverware. "Sit, sweetie. I made us breakfast."

Sarah sat, poured syrup on her pancakes, and took a bite. "These are great," she said. "You've finally done it."

"Done what?"

"Earned your five-star rating on Yelp."

"Wow. Only took two years," Lindsey said with a smile.

"Better late than never."

"How are the paintings coming for your next show in New York?"

"Three done. Six more to go. I'll have them finished in time. It's still four months away. I'm hoping Cricket can watch the store and you can come with me this time."

"I'm planning on it. The new girl we hired is working out great. Oh, I forgot to tell you, we got some new trees in at the nursery. I thought maybe you could come by on Monday after work and we can pick one out together." As part owner of the Green Thumb, Lindsey got everything at cost. She took care of the plants, while Cricket did the bookkeeping and paperwork. "We need something that represents *us*. Perhaps a nice magnolia."

"Ooh. I would love that." She took another bite. "And have I mentioned lately that I love you?"

Lindsey tapped her chin. "I believe you have. But you can tell me again."

"I love you."

"I love you, too."

They finished eating and Sarah helped Lindsey load the dishwasher. Lindsey wrapped her arms around Sarah and kissed her. "I'm so lucky," she said.

"And why is that?"

"Cause, I think the figs are just about ripe."

Sarah laughed. "Oh, I thought maybe it was because of me."

"Yeah. That's what I meant. I'm so lucky to have you—*and* the figs are just about ripe. But you come first on my list of lucky things."

"Right back atcha," Sarah said.

"Want to come check them with me? The figs I mean."

"I would go to the ends of the earth with you."

"How about to the end of the yard?" Linsey said with a smile.

It was going to be a gorgeous day. The sun was bright with just enough clouds sweeping by to keep it from being too hot.

"How do you know when they're ripe?" Sarah asked.

"See how this one is drooping and it's soft to the touch." Lindsey picked it from the tree that was now almost six feet tall and took a bite. The sweet berry flavor filled her senses. She offered the other half to Sarah.

"Wow. That's so good."

"Told ya," Lindsey said with a laugh. She picked three more and brought them into the house. She set them on the counter next to a vase filled with pink roses Sarah had picked the day before, that were bathed in sunshine filtered through the kitchen window. The large windows were one of the things that had attracted them to the house. It looked out onto the yard that now boasted two fig trees from the cuttings that Lindsey had so lovingly rooted and several rose bushes that she'd dug up from Sarah's old house. The spirits of Lindsey's grandmother and Julie had accompanied them to this new place. And Lindsey wouldn't have had it any other way.

About the Author

Creativity for Joy Argento started young. She was only five, growing up in Syracuse, New York, when she picked up a pencil and began drawing animals. These days she calls Rochester home, and oil paints are her medium of choice. Her award-winning art has found its way into homes around the globe.

Writing came later in life for Joy. Her love of lesbian romance inspired her to try her hand at writing, and she found her first self-published novels well received. She is thrilled to be a part of the Bold Strokes family and has enjoyed their books for years.

Joy has three grown children who are making their own way in the world and six grandsons who are the light of her life.

Books Available from Bold Strokes Books

All Things Beautiful by Alaina Erdell. Casey Norford only planned to learn to paint like her mentor, Leighton Vaughn, not sleep with her. (978-1-63679-479-2)

Appalachian Awakening by Nance Sparks. The more Amber's and Leslie's paths cross, the more this hike of a lifetime begins to look like a love of a lifetime. (978-1-63679-527-0)

Dreamer by Kris Bryant. When life seems to be too good to be true and love is within reach, Sawyer and Macey discover the truth about the town of Ladybug Junction, and the cold light of reality tests the hearts of these dreamers. (978-1-63679-378-8)

Eyes on Her by Eden Darry. When increasingly violent acts of sabotage threaten to derail the opening of her glamping business, Callie Pope is sure her ex, Jules, has something to do with it. But Jules is dead…isn't she? (978-1-63679-214-9)

Head Over Heelflip by Sander Santiago. To secure the biggest prizes at the Colorado Amateur Street Sports Tour, Thomas Jefferson will do almost anything, even marrying his best friend and crush—Arturo "Uno" Ortiz. (978-1-63679-489-1)

Letters from Sarah by Joy Argento. A simple mistake brought them together, but Sarah must release past love to create a future with Lindsey she never dreamed possible. (978-1-63679-509-6)

Lost in the Wild by Kadyan. When their plane crash-lands, Allison and Mike face hunger, cold, a terrifying encounter with a bear, and feelings for each other neither expects. (978-1-63679-545-4)

Not Just Friends by Jordan Meadows. A tragedy leaves Jen struggling to figure out who she is and what is important to her. (978-1-63679-517-1)

Of Auras and Shadows by Jennifer Karter. Eryn and Rina's unexpected love may be exactly what the Community needs to heal the rot that comes not from the fetid Dark Lands that surround the Community but from within. (978-1-63679-541-6)

The Secret Duchess by Jane Walsh. A determined widow defies a duke and falls in love with a fashionable spinster in a fight for her rightful home. (978-1-63679-519-5)

Winter's Spell by Ursula Klein. When former college roommates reunite at a wedding in Provincetown, sparks fly, but can they find true love when evil sirens and trickster mermaids get in the way? (978-1-63679-503-4)

Coasting and Crashing by Ana Hartnett Reichardt. Life comes easy to Emma Wilson until Lake Palmer shows up at Alder University and derails her every plan. (978-1-63679-511-9)

Every Beat of Her Heart by KC Richardson. Piper and Gillian have their own fears about falling in love, but will they be able to overcome those feelings once they learn each other's secrets? (978-1-63679-515-7)

Grave Consequences by Sandra Barret. A decade after necromancy became licensed and legalized, can Tamar and Maddy overcome the lingering prejudice against their kind and their growing attraction to each other to uncover a plot that threatens both their lives? (978-1-63679-467-9)

Haunted by Myth by Barbara Ann Wright. When ghost-hunter Chloe seeks an answer to the current spectral epidemic, all clues point to one very famous face: Helen of Troy, whose motives are more complicated than history suggests and whose charms few can resist. (978-1-63679-461-7)

Invisible by Anna Larner. When medical school dropout Phoebe Frink falls for the shy costume shop assistant Violet Unwin, everything about their love feels certain, but can the same be said about their future? (978-1-63679-469-3)

Like They Do in the Movies by Nan Campbell. Celebrity gossip writer Fran Underhill becomes Chelsea Cartwright's personal assistant with the aim of taking the popular actress down, but neither of them anticipates the clash of their attraction. (978-1-63679-525-6)

Limelight by Gun Brooke. Liberty Bell and Palmer Elliston loathe each other. They clash every week on the hottest new TV show, until Liberty starts to sing and the impossible happens. (978-1-63679-192-0)

Playing with Matches by Georgia Beers. To help save Cori's store and help Liz survive her ex's wedding they strike a deal: a fake relationship, but just for one week. There's no way this will turn into the real deal. (978-1-63679-507-2)

The Memories of Marlie Rose by Morgan Lee Miller. Broadway legend Marlie Rose undergoes a procedure to erase all of her unwanted memories, but as she starts regretting her decision, she discovers that the only person who could help is the love she's trying to forget. (978-1-63679-347-4)

The Murders at Sugar Mill Farm by Ronica Black. A serial killer is on the loose in southern Louisiana and it's up to three women to solve the case while carefully dancing around feelings for each other. (978-1-63679-455-6)

Fire in the Sky by Radclyffe and Julie Cannon. Two women from different worlds have nothing in common and every reason to wish they'd never met—except for the attraction neither can deny. (978-1-63679-573-7)

A Talent Ignited by Suzanne Lenoir. When Evelyne is abducted and Annika believes she has been abandoned, they must risk everything to find each other again. (978-1-63679-483-9)

An Atlas to Forever by Krystina Rivers. Can Atlas, a difficult dog Ellie inherits after the death of her best friend, help the busy hopeless romantic find forever love with commitment-phobic animal behaviorist Hayden Brandt? (978-1-63679-451-8)

Bait and Witch by Clifford Mae Henderson. When Zeddi gets an unexpected inheritance from her client Mags, she discovers that Mags served as high priestess to a dwindling coven of old witches—who are positive that Mags was murdered. Zeddi owes it to her to uncover the truth. (978-1-63679-535-5)

Buried Secrets by Sheri Lewis Wohl. Tuesday and Addie, along with Tuesday's dog, Tripper, struggle to solve a twenty-five-year-old mystery while searching for love and redemption along the way. (978-1-63679-396-2)

Come Find Me in the Midnight Sun by Bailey Bridgewater. In Alaska, disappearing is the easy part. When two men go missing, state trooper Louisa Linebach must solve the case, and when she thinks she's coming close, she's wrong. (978-1-63679-566-9)

Death on the Water by CJ Birch. The Ocean Summit's authorities have ruled a death on board its inaugural cruise as a suicide, but Claire suspects murder and with the help of Assistant Cruise Director Moira, Claire conducts her own investigation. (978-1-63679-497-6)

Living For You by Jenny Frame. Can Sera Debrek face real and personal demons to help save the world from darkness and open her heart to love? (978-1-63679-491-4)

Mississippi River Mischief by Greg Herren. When a politician turns up dead and Scotty's client is the most obvious suspect, Scotty and his friends set out to prove his client's innocence. (978-1-63679-353-5)

Ride with Me by Jenna Jarvis. When Lucy's vacation to find herself becomes Emma's chance to remember herself, they realize that everything they're looking for might already be sitting right next to them—if they're willing to reach for it. (978-1-63679-499-0)

Whiskey and Wine by Kelly and Tana Fireside. Winemaker Tessa Williams and sex toy shop owner Lace Reynolds are both used to taking risks, but will they be willing to put their friendship on the line if it gives them a shot at finding forever love? (978-1-63679-531-7)

Hands of the Morri by Heather K O'Malley. Discovering she is a Lost Sister and growing acquainted with her new body, Asche learns how to be a warrior and commune with the Goddess the Hands serve, the Morri. (978-1-63679-465-5)

I Know About You by Erin Kaste. With her stalker inching closer to the truth, Cary Smith is forced to face the past she's tried desperately to forget. (978-1-63679-513-3)

Mate of Her Own by Elena Abbott. When Heather McKenna finally confronts the family who cursed her, her werewolf is shocked to discover her one true mate, and that's only the beginning. (978-1-63679-481-5)

Pumpkin Spice by Tagan Shepard. For Nicki, new love is making this pumpkin spice season sweeter than expected. (978-1-63679-388-7)

Rivals for Love by Ali Vali. Brooks Boseman's brother Curtis is getting married, and Brooks needs to be at the engagement party. Only she can't possibly go, not with Curtis set to marry the secret love of her youth, Fallon Goodwin. (978-1-63679-384-9)

Sweat Equity by Aurora Rey. When cheesemaker Sy Travino takes a job in rural Vermont and hires contractor Maddie Barrow to rehab a house she buys sight unseen, they both wind up with a lot more than they bargained for. (978-1-63679-487-7)